BOOK THREE: THE DANGER

DIVE

**A world of adventure from
Gordon Korman**

DIVE

BOOK ONE: THE DISCOVERY
BOOK TWO: THE DEEP
BOOK THREE: THE DANGER

EVEREST

BOOK ONE: THE CONTEST
BOOK TWO: THE CLIMB
BOOK THREE: THE SUMMIT

ISLAND

BOOK ONE: SHIPWRECK
BOOK TWO: SURVIVAL
BOOK THREE: ESCAPE

www.scholastic.com

www.gordonkorman.com

GORDON KORMAN

BOOK THREE: THE DANGER

DIVE

AN
APPLE
PAPERBACK

SCHOLASTIC INC.
New York Toronto London Auckland Sydney
Mexico City New Delhi Hong Kong Buenos Aires

ISBN 0-439-50724-3

12   8/0

Printed in the U.S.A.   40

First printing, August 2003

For Chris and Kyle Kovalik

DIVE

07 September 1665

The black wave curled high above the Griffin, *and came crashing down on the barque with a roar like a wild beast. Tons of water washed over the streaming deck. As the bow was hammered down, the stern snapped high in the air with enough sudden violence that men were hurled off the ship to disappear into the raging sea. Such was the nature of the great storm that pounded His Majesty's privateer fleet in the autumn of 1665.*

Young Samuel Higgins was still aboard the Griffin *when she righted herself. But this was only because he had been lashed to a bulwark by York, the ship's barber and medical officer. York had been ordered by Captain James Blade to see to the welfare of the thirteen-year-old cabin boy. The barber took this responsibility seriously. Seamen who disappointed the* Griffin's *cruel master often felt the bite of his bone-handled snake whip.*

The sails were down to bare poles, and the captain himself had hold of the wheel. He steered his vessel straight into the wind, howling curses at the gale.

THE DANGER

2

"You'll not stop me, by God! The Griffin will yet ride low with a belly full of Spanish gold! No storm can change that!"

There was a crash as loud as a cannon shot, and the mizzenmast snapped clean in two. One hundred feet up, the top of the pole — thick as a century oak — began its plunge to the deck below.

Samuel tried to run, but the same tether that had saved him from being pitched overboard now prevented his flight. He was trapped — trapped in the path of hundreds of pounds of falling wood. A scream was torn from his throat, but it disappeared into the shrieking of the relentless wind.

The hurtling mast struck the tangle of ratlines and rigging, halting its destructive drop less than a handspan from Samuel's head.

Lucky. That was his nickname among the crew.

But no amount of luck would save him if the Griffin foundered in the onslaught of nature's wrath.

CHAPTER ONE

Star Ling came awake with a start, and stared at her unfamiliar surroundings. The room was an undecorated stark white, with one bed — her in it — and one chair — empty. An antiseptic smell permeated the air.

A hospital?

Investigating a stinging feeling, she noted that her hand was bandaged, and a tube protruded from the taped wrapping. Her eyes followed it all the way up to a plastic bag of clear fluid that hung from an IV pole by the side of the bed. She also felt the pure oxygen being administered through a nasal tube.

Am I sick?

There was a whoop in the hallway outside. "She's awake!"

In barged Bobby Kaczinski, Dante Lewis, and Adriana Ballantyne — Star's dive partners. The sight of their familiar faces triggered an avalanche of memory.

Their summer internship at Poseidon Oceanographic Institute had led the four teen divers to the site of a seventeenth-century shipwreck off the

THE DANGER

Caribbean island of Saint-Luc. When their discovery pointed to the existence of a second wreck in much deeper water, they had gone to investigate in *Deep Scout,* Poseidon's research sub.

Star remembered that. And then . . . the accident. She closed her eyes tightly to keep the tears from coming, and knew the answer before posing the hopeful question:

"Did I dream it all? The captain?"

"It was no dream," Kaz confirmed sadly.

Captain Braden Vanover had been their friend and mentor. When everyone else at Poseidon had treated the interns like unwanted excess baggage, he had spoken up for them, taken them under his wing. He had been at *Deep Scout's* controls when the submersible had failed. It was due to his skill alone that any of them had survived.

"Did we kill him?" moaned Star.

"I ask myself that a thousand times an hour," said Adriana in a broken voice. "I haven't got an answer."

Dante was devastated. "It's my fault. I'm the one who found the first wreck — and the trail leading to the second one." Dante's unusually sharp eyesight was the result of his color blindness. He saw only black, white, and shades of gray, but very little escaped him.

"Don't flatter yourself, Dante," Star told him in a voice that was weak, but very much her own. "You're not that important."

He looked down, embarrassed, and mumbled, "It's good to have you back. They said you might not make it. And after what happened to the captain — "

Star had a vision of Vanover's drowned body, sinking slowly. She had not known that he was already dead. Her attempts to save him had drawn her too deep for too long. An emergency ascent had brought on decompression sickness — the bends — the most deadly of all diving hazards.

Star could not remember what happened after that. "Where am I?" she asked.

"Brace yourself," Adriana advised. "You're about sixty stories above the open ocean, in the infirmary of the main oil-drilling platform. They brought you here by helicopter to a decompression chamber."

"Well, it worked," said Star. "Believe it or not, I feel pretty good — except I have to go to the bathroom, big-time!"

She swung her legs over the side of the bed, and stepped down to the floor. The room spun, and she hit the linoleum, face-first.

Adriana screamed loud enough to wake the dead. *"Nurse!"*

THE DANGER

White-coated staff came running.

Star sat up, her eyes wide and frightened. "I can't walk!"

The doctor on duty was the last to appear. "Ah, you are awake."

Two orderlies lifted her bodily and put her back onto the bed.

"Doctor, what's happening to me?" Star cried out. "My legs won't work!"

"Your legs are just fine," he soothed. "It is your brain where the problem lies right now."

"What?" Star was aghast.

The doctor explained that the brain controls the body by sending signals along neural pathways. With the bends, the body is invaded by tiny bubbles of nitrogen gas that block some of the pathways. "Your brain will attempt to develop new ones," he concluded. "In some patients, this is more difficult than in others."

"What do you mean?" Kaz asked anxiously. "She'll walk again, right?"

"It is impossible to determine at this time," the doctor replied. "It depends on the individual and the degree of neurological damage."

"But I've got cerebral palsy!" Star blurted. "I limp already!"

The doctor blinked. He hadn't been on duty

when Star had been treated. "And you're here on a *dive* internship?"

"She's the best diver around!" Adriana put in. "I mean, she *was* — " She fell silent.

The doctor considered this information. "It may complicate matters," he admitted. "Then again, perhaps the same tenacity that made you a diver despite the odds will help your recovery. But your diving career is at an end. You understand this, yes?"

No more diving! Right now it didn't seem like such a big deal, in view of Captain Vanover's death, and with her own future in doubt. But diving had always been more than a hobby for Star Ling. Once in the water, she had no handicap. Without her diving, she would be nothing more than the girl with the limp.

Stop it! she ordered herself. *Be happy. You're alive! You could be dead like the captain. . . .*

"And now," said the doctor to the three visitors, "I think it is time to let your friend get some rest."

Shattered, Kaz, Dante, and Adriana headed for the door.

"We'll be right outside," promised Adriana. "Just call — "

"Actually," the doctor interrupted, "I believe

THE DANGER

Dr. Gallagher wants you back at Poseidon."

"That would be a first," Kaz said bitterly.

In the fluorescent-lit corridor, Adriana let out a long breath. "Wow."

"She'll walk again," Kaz vowed, convincing himself as much as the others. "Star's tough. I'll bet she's more upset about not being able to dive."

"No diving," echoed Dante. "Where do I sign up? I will *never* dive again. I might not even shower!"

"Like Poseidon would even let us dive," snorted Kaz. "What do you think Gallagher wants with us? To give us the boot, that's what."

"We should just leave anyway," muttered Dante. "Save them the trouble of kicking us out."

"I have no place to go," offered Adriana in a thready voice. "My parents are jet-setting around the Black Sea, and our house is closed up for the summer."

Kaz stuck out his jaw. "I'm not leaving till they force me out. I don't want that treasure anymore, but I'm sure not going to let Tad Cutter take it. If Cutter's team comes up with that loot, I'm going to be right here to shoot my mouth off to every newspaper and TV station from Martinique to Mars!"

Tad Cutter, from Poseidon's head office in San

Diego, was officially the scientist sponsoring the teen internships. But really, Cutter and his two partners were treasure hunters. These people had turned the entire internship program into a smoke screen to cover their hunt for the wreck of the Spanish galleon *Nuestra Señora de la Luz*.

"I don't want that treasure, either," said Dante. "I mean, I still sort of want it. But it'll kill me if Cutter gets it."

"Gallagher thinks he's such a genius," Adriana put in angrily, "but he's too dumb to notice there's a team of treasure hunters right under his nose. That's the guy who's going to make decisions about our lives."

"Gallagher's a total idiot," Kaz agreed grimly. "It's nuts even to waste our time talking about him. Who knows what could be going on in his very small mind?"

THE DANGER

CHAPTER TWO

Dr. Geoffrey Gallagher leaned close to his office mirror and snipped an offending hair from his left sideburn. As the star of the video documentary on Poseidon–Saint-Luc, it was important for him to look his best. Jacques Cousteau may have been a genius, but he was too short for the screen. And those hats! Geoffrey Gallagher would put a new face on oceanography.

He turned around and regarded the three Californians seated on his couch — Tad Cutter, Marina Kappas, and Chris Reardon from Poseidon–San Diego.

"Well, Tad, what happens now?" the director asked. "We send the kids home, and you and your people go back to California?"

Cutter seemed surprised. "Of course not!" With the interns gone, he would have no excuse to remain in the Caribbean to go after the treasure. "It was an accident, Geoffrey."

"You say that like someone dropped a tray in the commissary!" Gallagher exclaimed irritably. "A man is dead; an adolescent girl very nearly

DIVE

lost her life and may never walk again; and an eighteen-million-dollar piece of equipment is lying broken at the bottom of the sea! That's not an accident — that's a catastrophe!"

Marina spoke up. "Nobody's downplaying the seriousness of what happened. But why penalize the interns? You don't know them like we do. They're good kids."

Gallagher found himself nodding, not because he agreed with her, but because Marina Kappas was drop-dead gorgeous. He found it hard to concentrate when she was around.

"If anyone is to blame in all this," Reardon took up the argument, "it's Braden Vanover. He didn't deserve to die for it, but come on! What was he thinking?"

"I agree," said Gallagher. "Which brings up the question of where *you* were when all this was going on. Those kids were your responsibility."

"I didn't want to make a big deal out of it," Cutter admitted, "but Braden kind of hijacked the whole internship project. Come on, Geoffrey. If you were a kid, what would you rather do — drag a sonar tow over hundreds of square miles of reef, or go deep-ocean exploring in a high-tech submersible?"

It was an absolute lie. In fact, Captain

Vanover had taken an interest in the four interns only when he'd noticed that they were being completely ignored by Cutter and company.

But Gallagher didn't know that. He asked, "And the three healthy ones are still interested in diving?"

"Maybe after a few days," was Marina's judgment. "But even if all they want to do is lie around the beach and fish a little, have a heart and let them. They've been through a lot."

"You're right." Gallagher nodded. "Besides, to ship them home would leave the Ling girl here all alone. It would be a public relations nightmare if any of the kids started talking to the press. Better to keep them happy." A vaguely annoyed look came over his face. "I sent for them today. They didn't come. They wouldn't leave their friend."

There was a sharp rap at the door, and Menasce Gérard walked in.

"Hey, English," Cutter greeted him.

No one seemed less English than English, who even had difficulty making himself understood in that language. The six-foot-five native dive guide had that nickname because legend said his family was descended from an English shipwreck survivor hundreds of years earlier. The young man was an experienced diver who worked on the oil rigs across the island. He had also done the occasional job for Poseidon — more specifically, for Braden Vanover. English and the captain had been fast friends.

He ignored Cutter and his crew, and spoke to the director. "We just came back since one half hour," he reported in a voice heavy with exhaustion. "We do not find the body."

Marina spoke up. "I'm so sorry, English. I know you and Braden were close."

The guide silenced her with a single brooding glance. English knew the true nature of Cutter's work, and had nothing but contempt for treasure hunters.

"I dive again tomorrow, me," he went on, still speaking only to Gallagher. "After that" — he shrugged — "there is no point."

"We're all praying that you find him," said Gallagher sympathetically.

"This is *difficile*," English explained. "Very deep water, much time for decompression, and not so much time for looking. I ask for use Tin Man. Then I can search till I find."

Tin Man was the nickname for Poseidon's one-atmosphere diving suit. This highly advanced rigid suit maintained surface pressure at any depth. The diver could descend as deep as necessary, and stay as long as necessary. Physically, he or she would never have left the surface.

THE DANGER

"I'm sorry, English," the director said seriously, "but Tin Man is a vital part of what we do here at Poseidon. Scientists reserve its use months in advance. I'm afraid the answer has to be no."

The big man scorched him with eyes of fire. "*Alors,* I think maybe you do not pray as hard as you say."

CHAPTER THREE

Star threw off the covers and swung her legs over the side of the mattress. She paused as a sweat broke out all over her body. She'd been in some tough spots — many of them right here on Saint-Luc — but she couldn't recall fearing anything as much as she now feared putting her feet on the floor.

She recalled the doctor's words: "There is no physical therapy for what you have. Your legs are not damaged. The problem is in your brain. Only *you* can make yourself walk again."

Clinging to the bed rail with her left hand, she swung over and balanced herself on the right side with a death grip on the nightstand. Her feet touched the floor. The contact felt normal, familiar.

So far, so good. She let go.

The collapse was total. Both legs buckled. In the nick of time, she flung her arms wide and broke her fall.

A second later, Dante's excited voice was heard from the doorway. "I think she's getting better. She's doing push-ups!"

THE DANGER

"Tell me you're not as dumb as the things you say," Star pleaded breathlessly.

Dante and Adriana picked her up off the floor and helped her back into bed.

Adriana was sympathetic. "Still no good, huh?"

Star grimaced in disgust. "I'm lucky I didn't break both my wrists when I went down." She spied the duffel slung over Dante's shoulder. "Hey, thanks — you brought my stuff."

"Not only that," said Adriana with a grin. She unzipped a side pocket and pulled out a paper bag soaked through with grease. From it she took a dripping sandwich on a once-crusty bun. "It got a little soggy," she said apologetically. "We had to wait over an hour for the motor launch to come out to the rig."

Star's eyes shone. "A conch burger! You guys are awesome. The food on the oil rig is just a notch above poison. No wonder English is so crabby all the time. He probably eats his meals here." She attacked the sandwich with gusto while sifting through her belongings with her free hand.

"My dive log," she exclaimed, holding up a well-thumbed diary. Her face fell. "Oh, yeah. Ancient history." She shook out some articles of clothing, a toiletry bag, a Walkman, and a stack of dive magazines.

An ivory-white object about a foot long fell out onto the blanket beside her. "Hey. What'd you bring this for?"

It was a carved whalebone handle that Star herself had found in the 340-year-old wreckage of *Nuestra Señora de la Luz.* The initials *J.B.* were etched above a large dark stone that was obscured by coral growth. Adriana had e-mailed a photograph of the piece to her uncle, an antiquities expert with the British Museum. He had identified it as the handle of a walking stick or whip, definitely English in origin. This was puzzling, because *Nuestra Señora* was a Spanish galleon. Every other artifact brought up by either Cutter or the four interns had been of Spanish origin.

"It's safer here than it is at the Institute," Adriana reasoned. "Remember — Cutter searched our cabins. This could be the one thing he doesn't know about yet."

"Good point," said Star. "On the other hand, who cares? We're out of the treasure business. We're probably kicked off the island, right? What did Gallagher say?"

"That's the weirdest part," said Dante. "We

THE DANGER

can stay. We can even dive if we want to — fat chance! Doesn't it figure? Now that our summer's in ruins, Poseidon remembers we exist!"

"They just don't want to be sued, that's all," said Star. She indicated a bouquet of flowers on her nightstand. "You'll never guess who these are from. Gallagher! And he's flying my dad down here, all expenses paid. If I was home, I'd get him to clean my room, too. Jerk!"

"You *should* sue," put in Dante. "That way at least something good would come out of all this."

"I hope you're kidding," said Star darkly. "No one should make money off what happened to the captain."

"I miss him," Adriana said quietly. "It's weird being at Poseidon. I keep expecting to walk around a corner, and there he'll be."

There was a melancholy silence.

Star finished her lunch. "Well, I appreciate you guys coming by. Hey, where's Kaz?"

Menasce Gérard loaded the last of the tanks onto the deck of the *Francisco Pizarro* and hopped on board. He checked the labels again. Deep diving with scuba gear was a complicated affair. Several different breathing gas mixtures were required, and the slightest error would scrap the dive. *Alors,* this was the last realistic chance to find the captain's body. So one checked, and checked again.

Captain Janet Torrington looked down from her position in the *Pizarro's* wheelhouse. "All set, English?"

Before he could reply, running footsteps sounded on the dock, and a frantic voice called, "Hey! Wait up!" Kaz pounded onto the scene, his dive bag bouncing wildly against his shoulder.

He leaped aboard. "I'm going with you!"

English was furious. "You! You are going nowhere! Get off the boat, or I throw you off!"

"Captain Vanover was my friend, too!" Kaz exclaimed.

"*Vraiment?* Is this so? Then I wish he chooses his friends more carefully! Do you American teenagers think this is some Hollywood *scenario,* and you are John Wayne leading the pony soldiers? This is not an adventure, silly child! And when you return to your shopping malls and MTV, Braden will still be dead!"

Kaz matched him glare for glare, and said the only thing that came to his mind: "I'm Canadian."

"*Je m'excuse* if I do not stamp your passport!"

THE DANGER

"Look, you need me," Kaz argued. "I was there when the captain died. I might recognize something."

"Such as what, monsieur? That there was the water all around, and it was very deep? Pah!" The guide dismissed this with a sweep of his hand. "This detective work I do not need."

"You can't know that," Kaz persisted. "If you come back without the body, you'll never know if I might have seen it. And today has to be the last day because he's been down there forty-eight hours already and . . ."

The sentence was too awful for him to finish aloud. At the bottom of the ocean, the captain's body would join the ocean's ecosystem. It would soon be disfigured by the feeding of sea life.

"Do you understand this job you volunteer for?" English demanded angrily. "This is not a fun swim for looking at the fishies! Three hundred feet of water is between us and what we seek. Do you not know that you must wear the equipment that weighs more than you? Do you not know that you must breathe the special gases because air is poison at such pressure? Do you not know that every minute on the bottom means four minutes of decompression, if you do not want to end up like your friend Star, or worse?" He snorted in disgust. "What you do not know about this dive would fill the set of encyclopedias!"

Kaz did not back down. "I'll stick with you every step of the way. I'll do whatever you do. Come on, you've got to let me try."

Captain Torrington raised an eyebrow at the hulking guide. "I don't think he's going to leave."

Kaz played his trump card. "You blame us for what happened to the captain. Fine. If I get into trouble down there, it's exactly what I deserve."

English harrumphed. "I will instruct you how to do this thing. But I hope you pay attention like your life depends on it. Because it does, monsieur."

As the *Pizarro* cut through the chop on an uncharacteristically hazy and unsettled day, Kaz did his best to squeeze years of training into a single thirty-minute boat ride. He thought the parade of equipment would never end. He would be carrying three regulators, five tanks of different breathing mixtures, three lights — one in his hood, one on his wrist, and a backup in the pocket of his buoyancy compensator, or B.C.

"You think this is daytime?" asked English. "At three hundred feet, it is always night."

Kaz soon learned that a mixed-gas dive had

THE DANGER

as much in common with recreational scuba as a polar expedition had with a walk in the park. Even his wet suit would be inadequate. The light-weight rubber was fine protection from the scrapes and stings of a coral reef. But only a thick neoprene shell would insulate him from the bone-chilling cold of the depths.

I may be nice and warm down there, he reflected, zipping up the heavy material, *but here in the tropical heat, I'm going to melt!*

English loaded him down with enough gear to flatten a packhorse. Back home in Toronto, Kaz had been a hockey player. He was used to heavy padding and protection. But this was unbelievable. More than one hundred pounds of equipment hung on his fourteen-year-old frame. It was all he could manage to put together a string of stiff-legged steps to the dive platform as Captain Torrington dropped anchor.

The spot was directly over the last reported position of *Deep Scout.*

All at once, Kaz felt fear. Could he do this? His basic dive certification didn't cover a mixed-gas jump to three hundred feet.

English was also loaded down, but he moved on deck with ease and confidence. He noticed Kaz's unease. "It is not too late for change the mind," he said, almost kindly.

Kaz shook his head stubbornly and jumped down to the platform. His knees nearly buckled on impact.

"Bring Braden home," ordered Torrington.

They hit the waves.

THE DANGER

CHAPTER FOUR

A powerful current manhandled Kaz right away. He fumbled with his B.C. to descend from the worst of its strength. But he forgot his heavy gear, and plunged thirty feet in a few seconds, popping his ears painfully. At last, he stabilized. Surprisingly, the extra weight wasn't too bad underwater, although the thick neoprene wet suit gave him the feeling he'd been laminated.

With effort, he kicked over to join English, and the two headed down the braided rope toward an invisible destination. The depth made Kaz dizzy. His previous dives had been over the reef, with the bottom clearly visible when he entered the water. All he could see now was a void, and its infinite blueness grew darker as they descended through clouds of marine life.

Just as Kaz was beginning to feel the unnerving wooziness of nitrogen narcosis, English clapped him on the shoulder.

Tank change. Kaz switched his regulator from the compressed air in his wing bottles to one of the big eighty-cubic-foot canisters on his back. He spat out an unnerving mouthful of salt water, and inhaled the metallic tang of tri-mix. Instantly, the drunkenness disappeared. English had prepared him for this. The intoxicating effect came from the nitrogen in air being absorbed into the body. But with tri-mix, much of the nitrogen was replaced by helium. This would be the gas mixture they breathed while at depth.

Passing through 150 feet, English turned on his headlamp, projecting a cone of illumination in the darkening water. Kaz did the same, and the sea came alive around him. But they were still nowhere near the bottom.

Two hundred feet. The length of a regulation hockey rink. On skates, Kaz could have covered the distance in a few seconds. Yet the surface seemed miles away. Even the fish avoided this darker world, preferring to stay within reach of the sun's light.

Hockey. It amazed Kaz how much the memory still stung. The Ontario Minor Hockey Association finals. A hard body check, a freak accident. And a boy named Drew Christiansen was confined to a wheelchair for life. So much had happened — Captain Vanover's death, Star's injury. Yet this was still the recollection that haunted Kaz, that kept him up at night. The sport he loved, that he was good at, had turned him into a weapon.

That was what had brought him to Poseidon

THE DANGER

in the first place. Diving in the tropics — what could be farther from hockey in Canada? That was why he was here, under seven atmospheres of pressure, hooked up to a floating laboratory of equipment, breathing a chemist's concoction of exotic gases.

Two hundred fifty feet. At last, there it was. The sea floor. It was slanted sharply downward. This was the place where the Hidden Shoals dropped off to deeper ocean.

At 270 feet, the divers made themselves neutrally buoyant for the search. Kaz looked around helplessly. Topside, it had seemed like a simple task: Go down to the correct coordinates and recover the body. But now he took in the featureless expanse of the slope. Their headlamps carved ghostly ovals out of the darkness of the sandy incline.

The divers synchronized watches. Kaz knew they had only twenty-five minutes of bottom time. Even that would require nearly two hours of decompression before they could safely return to the surface from this depth. If they stayed down any longer, they would not have enough breathing gas to complete the decomp. Then they would face the same choice Star had: suffocation or the bends.

So there was a ticking clock behind the hiss of his regulator. Kaz played his light over the vast sameness of the bottom. He kept a nervous eye on English, who was criss-covering the gradient with methodical track lines. To get lost down here — Kaz couldn't even bring himself to think about it. But one thing was for certain: It would be a death sentence.

Less thinking and more searching. You've only got fifteen minutes left!

He could feel the cold now, too. A wet suit was, after all, wet. The penetrating chill of the ocean made him shiver. Due to the slope of the sea floor, he had to adjust buoyancy to parallel it. He watched the numbers on his depth gauge: 280 feet, 290. Would they reach three hundred? It seemed likely. This incline continued a long way. Aboard *Deep Scout*, the interns had spotted scattered debris in this area, leading down to the second shipwreck at seven hundred feet.

Another tank change. Kaz clipped his regulator into the second big eighty. Down here, gas disappeared at lightning speed, squeezed to practically nothing by nearly ten atmospheres of pressure. *Eleven minutes.*

Kaz's breath caught in his throat as English descended to investigate a dark shape on the

THE DANGER

bottom. But it was a false alarm — an area of black mud on the sandy gradient. Kaz checked his watch. *Four minutes.*

We let you down again, Captain, he thought in misery. *All you did was be nice to us, and you paid for it with your life. We can't even recover your body for a decent burial.*

He squandered his remaining time, barely kicking his flippers. What difference would it make if they found him? Braden Vanover, the man, the friend, would still be dead.

His dark eyes awash in anguish and fatigue behind his mask, English signaled their return to the anchor line. The search was over. Kaz began to cry softly, but he followed without argument. They ascended slowly, allowing their bubbles to outpace them.

As they passed through two hundred feet, the faint glow of Kaz's headlamp, weakened by the distance to the slope, fell upon a huge sea fan. It had doubled over under its own weight. Standing upright, the thing would have been seven feet tall.

A rush of adrenaline electrified Kaz's core, radiating outward to his extremities. The memories of that awful day exploded like a fragmentation grenade inside his brain, jump-cut images, a real-life music video: the roar of ocean flooding the dying sub, the struggle to get out, the panicked ascent. And, through the haze of nitrogen narcosis, a dark, murky picture — an enormous sea fan collapsed on the slope, just a few yards away.

Kaz broke off the anchor line, finning for the buckled fan.

"No!" cried English into his regulator.

The guide was going to kill him for this, and Kaz didn't really blame him. This detour could throw off their entire decompression schedule, a deadly risk. But something other than reason was propelling Kaz away from the rope and safety. There was one final slim chance to recover the captain, and Kaz had to take it.

He swam with all his might, gritted his teeth, and looked down.

THE DANGER

CHAPTER FIVE

The body was so close that Kaz recoiled in revulsion.

Captain Vanover lay upon the slope, still in the street clothes he had been wearing on *Deep Scout's* final voyage. The arms were in an outstretched position, swaying softly, matching the movement of the fan.

Calm down! Kaz ordered himself as his breathing began to accelerate. If he hyperventilated, he could inhale the rest of his tri-mix in no time at all.

Swallowing hard, he descended to the corpse. He watched as the face entered the cone of brightness provided by the headlamp. He had been prepared for a horror-movie image, a hideously disfigured carcass. But what he saw was perhaps even more disturbing. Although his complexion was blue and lifeless, Braden Vanover looked very much as he always looked — as if he were about to speak. To laugh out loud and tell them it was all a big joke.

It's no joke, Kaz thought tragically.

The eyes were closed. And when Kaz

reached out to touch Vanover's arm, the skin didn't feel like human flesh anymore. It was rubbery — the cold smoothness of neoprene.

English approached from above, his face a mixture of sorrow and triumph. Despite his emotions, he did not waste a single second. At this point, every bottled breath was borrowed from their vital decompression time.

The operation was not complicated. Kaz helped English carry the body — it was surprisingly buoyant — over to the anchor line. The guide attached two lift bags to his friend — one under each arm. Then he inflated the bags with shots of air from his B.C. The body rose up the rope as if by magic. It was out of sight almost immediately.

Back on the ascent, Kaz could only imagine the gruesome discovery awaiting Captain Torrington when the corpse reached its destination. As it rose, the air in its cavities would expand. The body had not been deformed in its watery grave, but on the surface it would be bloated beyond recognition.

Approaching one hundred feet, they switched back to compressed air. Kaz was aware of the pleasant drowse of narcosis, but the feeling had faded by the time English clutched the line and signaled for him to do the same. They had

THE DANGER

reached sixty feet — their first decompression stop.

The idea was that a deep diver could avoid the bends by returning to the surface slowly. This would allow absorbed gases to breathe out naturally rather than bubbling into the bloodstream and tissues. It was achieved by making five stops on the ascent.

The sixty-foot stop was short — four minutes of fish watching and thumb twiddling. But the times quickly grew. The twelve minutes at forty weren't so bad, but Kaz found himself staring at his dive watch during the eighteen minutes at thirty. Another problem: Up here the sea was warm, but their heavy neoprene suits were designed for much colder ocean. He was sweating profusely.

Finally, it was time for the twenty-foot stop. Here, the current was a factor once again. Kaz had to cling to the anchor line to maintain his position. It wasn't difficult at first, but the effort required to keep it up for the full thirty-two minutes was physically exhausting.

The depth isn't what gets you, he reflected. *It's the decomp that drives you mad!*

He was really dreading their final stop. It was right in the teeth of the current at ten feet. And it was scheduled to last *more than an hour.*

Plodding up the rope was like mountain climbing — inching hand over hand through an overpowering wind. When they reached the ten-foot mark, he held on for dear life, flapping like a flag in the fast-moving water. It was time to switch to their third and final breathing gas — pure oxygen to speed decompression.

But how can I change tanks in this current? If I let go with even one hand, I'm lost.

He tried calling into his mouthpiece. "I can't — "

English cut him off. "You *will*." Curling his right arm into an iron clamp around the line, he enfolded the boy in a bear hug with the left. Kaz struggled clumsily with the hoses, fumbling to clip the regulator in place. His first breath brought in only seawater. The coughing fit followed immediately. To be out of control, untethered from the rope, made his stomach leap up the back of his throat.

"Try again!" ordered English, eyes afire. "Vite!"

There it was. A clean snap this time, and the clear, strong taste of oxygen. Kaz grabbed the line once more. Sixty-four minutes to go.

The ache in his wrists grew to twisting agony. His fingers stiffened painfully, and then went

THE DANGER

numb. And the heat — he was quite literally swimming in his own perspiration inside the heavy rubber suit. When he dared to look at his watch, only eleven minutes had gone by.

Close your eyes. It helps the time pass.

But the darkness in his head only reminded him of the darkness of the deep, filling his mind with images of the captain's lifeless body listing on the slope.

And when he opened his eyes, he was looking straight at Clarence.

Kaz's very being convulsed with terror as he stared at the shadowy behemoth about twenty yards away. What else could it be but the eighteen-foot monster tiger shark of local legend? The sleek, muscular body, longer than many boats; the triangular dorsal fin; the top-heavy crescent tail; the huge, gaping mouth . . .

He was never actually aware of letting go of the anchor line. He felt the manhandling force of the current. But at that moment, his fear of the shark prevented him from realizing just how much trouble he was in. The water was conveying him away from Clarence — that was all he cared about just then.

"Boy!" shouted English, lunging for his charge.

Accelerating in the current, Kaz noticed for

the first time how huge the shark was — much larger than he remembered Clarence. He could also make out pale yellow markings on the dark gray skin, almost like polka dots. The mouth looked wrong, too, limp and floppy. The tiger shark had powerful jaws, capable of snapping a person in two.

The truth came to Kaz in a moment of horror. This wasn't Clarence at all! This was a twenty-five-foot whale shark — a huge but harmless plankton eater.

He had let go of the anchor line — the *lifeline* — for *nothing*.

Menasce Gérard watched Kaz's receding form disappear in the surging current. He had no doubt that he could catch up to the boy. But then the two of them would be lost, with no way to call for rescue. No, the only course of action was to remain here; to remain calm. He would complete his decompression, return to the *Pizarro*, and then go after the boy.

Mon dieu, those teenagers were trouble. Yet he had to admit that without Kaz, they never would have recovered the captain's body. *Oui*, he owed the boy that. His stubborn insistence on joining this expedition was as courageous as it was foolhardy.

THE DANGER

English regarded his watch. He still had more than forty minutes to go, but he could cut that time in half. It was risky, but necessary to rescue the boy.

Twenty nervous minutes later, he broke the surface. Not wanting to risk even a short swim in the powerful current, he hauled himself and his equipment straight up the anchor line, and swung a long leg over the gunwale of the *Pizarro.*

Vanover's remains had already been placed inside a gray body bag on the deck. Perhaps that was best — to remember Braden as he was, not in this state.

But this was a time for action, not reflection.

"That was fast," commented Captain Torrington. "Where's Kaz?"

English kicked away his flippers and flung off his equipment. "The Zodiac! *Vite!*"

Torrington did not ask questions. In the few seconds it took for the guide to scramble out of his dripping wet suit, she had the inflatable raft on the dive platform, ready for launch. She suggested one change of plan. "You must be exhausted. Let me look for him."

English shook his head. "I let him dive, me. He is on my conscience." He tossed the Zodiac into the water and stepped inside. As the outboard motor roared to life, he looked around helplessly. Kaz had been drifting for almost half an hour.

Who could guess how far away the boy might be?

THE DANGER

CHAPTER SIX

Tired.

Kaz's awareness diminished one wave at a time, until only that single word remained.

He bobbed in the heavy chop, kept afloat by the air in his B.C. But he felt nothing anymore — no motion, no spray, no heat from the blazing sun. He knew only his own exhaustion.

His sense of time had been the first to go. Underwater, fighting the current, he had lost track of the decompression schedule. Terrified of ascending too soon, he'd done the only thing that made any sense — stayed under until his oxygen had run out. At that point, he'd had no choice. He had broken the waves, gasping for air.

He had no idea how long he'd been floating here. Hours? *Days?* The one thing he knew with absolute clarity was that it couldn't go on much longer.

He struggled against the confusion, reciting his name, address, and telephone number — concrete facts to replace his disorientation.

DIVE

"My name is Bobby Kaczinski . . . I play right defense . . ."

Then what are you doing in the middle of the ocean?

It took a moment for him to come up with the answer to that question.

"I'm a diver. I was on a dive, but something went wrong." He could not remember what, just that he was here, and had been here for a long time.

He barely noticed when the roar of the outboard motor swelled over the whitecaps. Nor did he recognize the dark features that loomed over him as he was lifted into the inflatable raft. But the face of his rescuer was the most welcome sight he'd ever laid eyes on.

Adriana and Dante hurried through the narrow streets of the tiny village of Côte Saint-Luc.

They had ridden their bikes back from the oil rig where they'd spent the afternoon with Star. At Poseidon, they'd been greeted by a message taped to Dante's cabin door: *Boy is at my home.*

It was signed Menasce Gérard.

"What's Kaz doing at English's place?" Dante

queried as they passed the bar and grill where they had bought Star's lunch many hours before. "Do you suppose he's got a dungeon in there somewhere?"

"That was no easy dive they went on today," Adriana reminded him. "I'll bet Kaz did well, and English is having him over for dinner. We might be invited, too."

"That guy hates our guts," grumbled Dante. "If he's having us for dinner, it's because we're the main course."

She swallowed hard, afraid to say it out loud. "Do you think they found the captain?"

"I sure hope so. I don't like the idea of him lost down there."

English lived in a tiny cottage in the center of town. The big dive guide answered their knock, scowling as usual. They looked beyond him to where Kaz sat in a high-backed rattan chair, drinking from a steaming mug.

Adriana stared. Kaz's face gleamed with a thick coating of cream covering an angry red sunburn. "What happened to you?"

"Nothing," said Kaz. "I'm okay."

"But how'd you get roasted underwater?" Dante persisted.

"I lost the anchor line during decomp," Kaz

explained. "Drifted for a while. But we found the captain."

"Thank God," Adriana breathed.

English spoke up. "This ointment is the best remedy. There is an old woman in the hills who makes it. Also the tea. Good for the dehydration."

"Don't ask me to describe the taste," Kaz added sourly.

"So what happens now?" Dante asked English. "With the captain, I mean."

"The body will be shipped to his sister in Florida." The dark eyes flashed bitter resentment at them. "You are maybe surprised there is no miracle cure for three days drowned?"

Adriana felt instant tears spring to her eyes. "You blame us for his death, don't you?"

The dive guide didn't answer right away. Then he said, "I blame only the bad luck. But if you do not come to my island, Braden, he is still alive, yes?"

"We're so sorry," she barely whispered. "He was really good to us."

"I think you take your friend and go now." It was not a suggestion; they were being dismissed.

THE DANGER

Kaz stood up. "You probably saved my life — again."

"It was you who found Braden," English said grudgingly. He looked over to where Adriana, always the archaeologist, was staring at the weathered wooden carving of an eagle's head and wings that hung in a fishnet in the window of the small cottage. "And you, mademoiselle," he added impatiently. "What may I say that might drive you away from me and my property?"

Kaz spoke up. "Give her a break."

"This piece," Adriana persisted. "I e-mailed a picture of it to my uncle, and he thinks it might be just as old as some of the other stuff we found."

English sighed. "If I explain you this thing, you will leave, yes?"

"Please," said Adriana, flushed with embarrassment.

"The story of my supposed-to-be English ancestor — after the shipwreck, he floated to Saint-Luc on this wood."

The girl's eyes shone with excitement. "Uncle Alfie said the piece probably broke off a ship, because the back is all jagged! And the wood definitely doesn't come from here!"

English was unimpressed. "This is family legend only — probably not true. And now you will do me the favor to go home."

Kaz paused at the door. "It was worth it — going after the captain, I mean. I'm glad we found him."

"I, too, am glad," said Menasce Gérard.

08 September 1665

*Samuel came awake to the strong taste of rum be-
ing forced down his throat. He gagged.*

*"Drink it, Samuel," ordered York. "It'll clear
your head." Once again the burning liquid was
forced past his lips.*

*Choking and spitting, he sat up and leaned back
against the bulwark. He would have vomited, too,
had there been anything in his belly. For three days,
the crew of the Griffin had battled the storm. There
had been no time for eating or sleeping with the de-
struction of the ship so close at hand.*

*The storm. That was what was different now. The
tempest had passed, praise heaven. The rain had
ceased, the wind was down, and the sea was calm.
But the Griffin — the barque looked like the after-
math of a battle. Ropes and debris littered the deck.
The mizzenmast had been snapped in half, and a
loose starboard cannon had smashed through planking and partially collapsed a companionway.*

*The cabin boy's eyes turned to York. The barber's
white smock was spattered with blood. Amputations*

of broken or crushed limbs, *thought Samuel. The pungent smell of burned flesh filled the air. Stumps sealed, wounds cauterized, all to prevent an infection that would very likely come anyway.*

The feeling of hopelessness that washed over Samuel was becoming more and more familiar. His had not been a happy life — he had been kidnapped from his family at the age of six, and had worked as a chimney sweep before running away to sea. Yet the despair that visited him now was sharper than what he remembered from his deprived childhood. Fear of dying was not nearly as unpleasant as fear of living. The captain and crew of the Griffin *were privateers — licensed pirates. Murderers, torturers, thieves. The world would have been a finer place had the ship and all hands gone down in the gale.*

"Any idea where we are, sir?" Samuel asked listlessly.

"None at all, sad to say," the barber told him. "Separated from the fleet and leagues off course. 'Twill be a miracle if any of us see home again. Now shake a leg. The captain's cabin needs tidying after the storm."

James Blade's quarters were in a frightful state. He was not a neat man to begin with, hurling objects in his terrible temper, and letting dropped items lie where they fell. The storm had added to this disarray. Possessions and bedclothes were strewn about the

THE DANGER

deck space, and a crystal decanter of brandy had shattered. Books had toppled from the shelving and lay open, the paper soaking up the brown liquid.

Samuel rescued the books first, out of a feeling that they were more precious than anything else in the room. Although he could not understand the strange symbols on their pages, he suspected that the volumes revealed a world less harsh than this one. A world where life held more than suffering, violence, and greed.

Lying in the twisted bed linens was the captain's snake whip, its baleful emerald eye glowing from its setting in the carved whalebone handle. Samuel drew back. This was the object he hated more than any other — almost as much as he hated Captain Blade himself. The image of Evans the sail maker, Samuel's only friend, brought tears to the cabin boy's eyes. The poor old man had tasted this whip many times. Those floggings had brought on the terrible circumstances in which Blade had pushed Evans to his death.

He was about to make up the captain's berth when the cry came:

"Sail ho!"

A ship! The fleet!

By the time Samuel reached the companionway, seamen were flocking to the port gunwale, and an excited babble rose from the deck. Samuel joined the *rush, careful to avoid stepping on the rats that any shipboard stampede was sure to stir up.*

Captain Blade strode to the rail. "Well, come on, man! Is she one of ours?"

"She's square-rigged, sir! I'm looking for a marking."

With a practiced flick of the wrist, Blade snapped open his brass spyglass and put it to his eye.

"A galleon, by God! She's a Spaniard!"

York pushed his way forward. "One of the treasure fleet?"

"Aye!" roared the captain. "Storm-damaged and helpless. Take up your swords, lads! This night we'll be counting our plunder!"

THE DANGER

CHAPTER SEVEN

Star sat up in bed and swung her legs over the side, her features set in an expression of grim determination.

I will not be crippled by this. I had a disability before, and it didn't stop me. This isn't going to beat me, either.

But her legs buckled instantly, and no force of will could straighten them. A flailing arm tried to catch the nightstand, but succeeded only in up-ending the duffel bag that sat there. The pain that came when her shoulder made contact with the hard floor was nothing compared with the anguish in her heart.

I didn't expect to tap-dance today, but shouldn't there be some sign of improvement? Some ray of hope that I'm getting better? Something?

Enraged, she picked up the first thing her hand closed on — the bone handle. With a cry, she hurled it with all her might across the room. With a crack, it struck the steel door frame and bounced off.

All at once, her anger turned inward. *Sure,*

that makes sense. Smash a three-hundred-year-old artifact. That'll help you walk.

Now the only piece from the shipwrecks that Cutter didn't know about was lying on the floor like a dropped pencil. She had to hide it away before anybody saw it.

Using her arms, which were swimmer-strong, she began to pull herself across the tiles. Panting, she reached for the hilt. It was just out of her grasp.

"Room 224," came a familiar voice from outside in the reception area.

Oh, no, Marina Kappas!

In a desperate bid, Star stretched her body to full extension, snatched up the carved whalebone, and wriggled back toward the bed. There were footsteps in the hall as she stashed the handle back in the duffel, zipped it shut, and shoved it under the nightstand.

Two legs appeared in the doorway. "Star, what are you doing on the floor?" the striking Californian asked in alarm.

"The Australian crawl," Star replied sarcastically. "What does it look like I'm doing? I'm trying to walk, and it isn't happening."

And then a soft voice spoke her name.

For the first time, she looked up. "Dad," she barely whispered.

THE DANGER

So much had happened in the past weeks, but their exotic location had given it a dreamlike fairy-tale quality. Now, to see her father — someone from home, from her real life — brought it all crashing down on her.

It was heartbreaking and terrifying at the same time.

Mr. Ling scooped his daughter off the floor and lifted her gently back to her bed. There he held her and let her cry.

Zipped safely away in the duffel bag, the whalebone handle rested on a pile of wadded-up T-shirts. What Star had been in too much of a hurry to notice was that the collision with the door frame had chipped a piece of coral from the hilt. The stone set in its center now glowed a deep fiery green.

The crane was so large that, when its winch was in operation, the roar was like an airport runway during takeoff. Poseidon Oceanographic Institute had nothing like it. This titanic piece of equipment, along with *Antilles IV*, the enormous ship that supported it, was on loan from Antilles Oil Company. It was normally used to salvage lost drill parts and underwater piping. But today the quarry was *Deep Scout*, the research submersible that had been disabled and abandoned by the late Captain Vanover and the four interns.

Three hundred feet below, oil company divers fastened grappling hooks and lift bags to the crippled sub's hull. And then the powerful cables began to haul *Deep Scout* from its watery prison. The lift bags inflated as the vehicle rose and the air inside expanded.

Minutes later, *Deep Scout* broke the surface, its clear bubble gleaming in the sun. Dripping, it was winched onto the expansive work bed of the *Antilles IV*, where dozens of crew members awaited it.

Far astern, a second, smaller crane was in operation. It was raising the diving bell, which housed the salvage divers. It also acted as a decompression chamber, saving the deep-sea workers the need to make decompression stops in the water.

Inside the bell, the men played cards, read magazines, and snoozed the time away. But one pair of eyes was glued to the porthole, following the progress of the work on *Deep Scout*.

English watched intently as the crew shoveled an endless supply of wet mud out of the sub's belly. *Oui*, this was in agreement with what the four teenagers had told him. Two fiberglass plates had separated, causing *Deep Scout* to scoop up huge quantities of sand and mud from the ocean

THE DANGER

floor. The extra weight had made the vehicle too heavy to return to the surface.

English and his fellow divers were used to decomps that lasted up to two weeks, but today their stay was short. After two and a half hours, the bell was opened, and the deep-water crew emerged. By this time, the sub's titanium husk was suspended above the salvage deck. A single technician stood below, examining the vehicle and making notes on a clipboard.

English went to join him, peering up at the short, snub-nosed hull. He spotted the loose plates almost at once.

He pointed. "Here — this was the problem, yes?"

The man nodded. "The temperature gauge is behind there." He frowned. "I can't imagine how the plates came apart. It's never happened before, and this boat's fifteen years old."

The native guide squinted for a better look. According to the interns, the damage had been done by a collision with the shark Clarence. But, *alors*, this seemed unlikely. The attack of a large tiger shark would batter the fiberglass, leaving dents from the rounded snout. These panels were intact except for the locking mechanism, which was bent apart.

A one-in-a-million shot from an angry predator?

No. Then the connection would be bent *inward*. This was bent *outward* — almost as if it had been pried apart. . . .

"Sabotage?" he mused aloud.

The technician laughed. "What for? Who would go after a research sub? It's got nothing but bottom samples and rare algae."

It took a lot to surprise Menasce Gérard, but when his mind made the leap, he was profoundly shocked. Perhaps other missions were seeking sand and algae. But on this occasion, *Deep Scout* had been after sunken treasure.

Who had an interest in seeing that mission fail?

For Tad Cutter and his crew, frustration had begun to set in. They had been excavating the wreck site on the reef, and knew it to be the fabled galleon *Nuestra Señora de la Luz*. They had found a great many artifacts there — dishes, cutlery, medallions, crucifixes, weapons, and ammunition; even huge items like anchors and cannon barrels. There was only one problem. An estimated $1.2 billion in Spanish treasure was simply not there.

THE DANGER

That amount of silver, gold, and gems didn't merely get up and walk away. It was definitely down there somewhere. But where to look for it? That was the question.

The kids seemed to be after the treasure, too, with Braden Vanover helping them. But why had they taken a submersible into deep water when the shipwreck was right there on the reef, a mere sixty-five feet beneath the waves? Did the kids know something that Cutter didn't?

It was infuriating, and not a little worrisome. The Californians hadn't been out on the R/V *Ponce de Léon* in days. Their excavation was a dead end, but what were they supposed to do? Start from scratch?

Bide their time. That was Marina's idea. But how long could they keep this up before Gallagher noticed that they weren't mapping the reef anymore? How many hours could Cutter waste in the Poseidon laundry room, watching his socks tumbling by in the window of the dryer and praying for a jolt of inspiration?

The machine clicked off, and Cutter listlessly began to fold his clothes.

The laundry room door was pushed open so violently that it slammed into the wall, and English burst onto the scene, his face a thundercloud.

"English — what brings you — ?"

The guide crossed the room in two strides that would have been impossible for a normal-sized person. In a single motion, he pulled a large towel out of Cutter's basket, wrapped it around the smaller man's torso, and pulled tight, binding his arms to his sides.

Cutter was shocked. "What's going on, man?"

His rage boiling over, English squeezed harder. "You will tell me how you killed Braden Vanover, monsieur, and I maybe take you to the police alive!"

Cutter was having trouble breathing. "What are you talking about? Nobody killed Braden! It was a sub accident! The shark — "

"*Enough!*" The diver's booming voice rattled every loose object in the room. "I see this 'accident.' Unless the shark is handy with the crowbar, this is no accident! This is *le sabotage*! And who has the motive for this? *You!*"

The look of astonishment on Cutter's face was so complete that English released him at once. Surely such genuine surprise could not be faked.

"You're *serious*?" Cutter was aghast. "Someone tampered with the sub? And you think it was me?"

"I am not blind, me," English growled. "Do you think you can hide from me this thing you do? I see the coral you destroy to search for gold. I see you smash the reef with airlift and jackhammer. You do not fool me!"

"Okay, okay," said Cutter. "We're not saints. But we're not killers, either."

English glared at him. "We shall see." He turned on his heel and left as abruptly as he had arrived.

CHAPTER EIGHT

Chris Reardon was horrified. "He accused you of *murder?*"

Cutter sat back in his chair in the small office space Poseidon had assigned to the team from California. "Pretty much. He said the sub was sabotaged, and that's what killed Braden and got the girl bent. I think — I *hope* — I convinced him we didn't do it."

The bearded man shuddered. "English! I wouldn't want to have that guy mad at me."

"We already do," Cutter said morosely. "He's figured out what we're doing here. For some reason, he's keeping his mouth shut, or Poseidon would have bounced us by now."

"He probably doesn't talk to Gallagher," Reardon observed. "Either that or he knows we haven't found one red cent in that lousy wreck."

Marina breezed into the office, waving a videocassette. "Hey, guys, ready for movie night?"

"It's three o'clock in the afternoon," grumbled Reardon.

"What's that?" asked Cutter.

THE DANGER

Marina flashed all thirty-two perfect teeth. "Nothing much — just a copy of the tape from *Deep Scout*'s onboard camera."

Reardon was astonished. "How'd you get that?"

"The chief engineer in charge of the investigation — turns out he likes me." She favored her two partners with a supermodel smile. "You want to know what Braden and the kids were looking for? If they found it, it's on here."

Cutter snatched the tape from her hand and popped it into the VCR on the desk. "Shut the door."

The three treasure hunters huddled around the small TV screen. *Deep Scout*'s camera was triggered automatically as soon as the sub was in water. The monitor showed a steady descent from pale turquoise water, teeming with fish, to depths beyond the reach of the sun's rays. It recorded the instant when the sub's floodlights came on, and even the reaction of a startled octopus.

A counter on the top right kept track of elapsed time on the dive. Below that was a depth readout. By following the numbers, they could see that the descent to three hundred feet was quick and direct. But then the sub leveled off and began what appeared to be track lines along the sloped ocean floor.

"They're looking for something," Reardon murmured.

"This must be just past the excavation," Cutter decided, "where the shoal drops off."

They watched the sub's lights play back and forth over the sandy incline for a few minutes. Marina hit FAST FORWARD, and they began to scan the tape at greater speed. The search continued for quite a while, and suddenly Cutter hit PAUSE.

"Look at that!"

All three stared. It was badly corroded and half buried in the sand, but it was easily identified: a cannon barrel.

"Keep going," ordered Marina. "Let's see what else there is."

The Californians watched in awe as the ocean bottom gave up its secrets before their very eyes. Beyond the cannon, a vast debris field opened up, stretching hundreds of feet down the gradient.

The silence in the room was total, because none of the three was breathing.

"That's impossible!" Reardon blurted finally. "The wreck is on the reef, under tons of coral! How did this stuff get all the way down here to" — he checked the readout — "five hundred feet?"

"Deeper," amended Marina, her eyes glued to the monitor. "Look."

THE DANGER

It was true. Not only did the debris continue down the slope, but there seemed to be more of it the farther the sub descended.

"This is unreal!" Cutter exclaimed, more as a complaint than anything else. "I'm looking right at it, but I can't believe my eyes."

And then came a full view of what *Deep Scout's* occupants had seen before the accident. Far below the surface, lodged on a muddy shelf at 703 feet, the debris field came to an abrupt end in the remains of a ship.

To three trained treasure hunters, the sight was unmistakable. Even some of the wooden ribs of the old hull were visible, packed in the wet sand.

"*Another* ship?" Reardon exclaimed in consternation. "That's impossible!"

"Which one is *Nuestra Señora*?" asked Cutter.

"Who cares?" snapped Marina. "The treasure's not up on the reef. It stands to reason that it must be down there."

Reardon stared at her. "Are you going to dive to seven hundred feet?"

"There are ways," Marina reminded him.

"There's a time factor here, too," the team leader pointed out. "We're just finding out about this. The kids have known for a week."

"The kids wouldn't dare," said Reardon. "After what happened to them, they won't even be stepping in puddles, let alone diving."

"Maybe not," said the team leader, "but they can still talk. Braden may be gone, but there are plenty of other people on this island who could find a use for a billion dollars."

Marina hit STOP, and the screen went blank. "Speaking of poor Braden, some of the locals are putting on a memorial service on the beach tonight. We can't miss it."

Cutter turned pale. "Are you crazy? I can't go to that! English thinks I killed the guy!"

"All the more reason why we have to be there," she argued. "We've come so far, and we're so close. Let's not lose sight of the prize just when it's in our reach."

THE DANGER

CHAPTER NINE

It was not yet dark, but the bonfire was flaming high into the dusky sky over the beach at Côte Saint-Luc. About forty people were in attendance when the three interns made their way in from the road, hanging back where the mangroves gave way to the flat sand.

Dante, whose color blindness also gave him excellent night vision, squinted at the crowd.

"Who's there?" asked Adriana. "A lot of institute people?"

"All I see is English. He's twice as big as everybody else. The second we get there, he's going to give us the boot."

"Gallagher?" asked Kaz.

"I don't think so," Dante reported.

"Jerk," muttered Adriana. "He won't come to pay his respects because fixing *Deep Scout* is going to cost Poseidon money."

The crowd was mixed. There were sailors and scientists from the institute, and quite a few locals as well. The atmosphere was more subdued than a party, but it was no funeral, either. People

DIVE

talked quietly, sharing reminiscences of Braden Vanover, and adding mementos to a small table where pictures of the late captain were displayed. There was even occasional laughter, as the memories were often funny.

As the three teenagers joined the group, the first familiar face they encountered belonged to Marina Kappas.

"Thanks for coming, guys," she greeted them. "It means a lot. What do you hear from Star?"

"She's not good," Dante admitted, dazzled by the dark-haired beauty. "They've got a physiotherapist working with her, but she's still not walking. Mr. Ling wants to take her home to the States."

"What a terrible accident." Marina's voice was warm with sympathy. "Braden gone, and Star — "

"Star will be just fine," Adriana said curtly.

"Come on, Adriana — " Kaz began.

"No, you come on!" The girl had never been one to look for a fight. But right now she was picturing Star standing with them. Star had always been suspicious of Marina's outward show of friendliness. Cutter and his crew were not their friends. Magazine-cover looks did not change that fact.

THE DANGER

"Don't pretend you care about Star," Adriana told Marina bluntly. "Don't pretend you care about any of us." And she literally marched Kaz and Dante away from the Californian, past Cutter and Reardon, and over to the crackling bonfire.

"You're right, you know," Dante said to Adriana. "Star would have done the same thing."

"Star would have bitten her head off," Kaz amended with just a touch of pride. He added wistfully, "Star belongs here more than anybody. She was trying to save the captain when she got herself bent."

The three interns were saying hello to Captain Janet Torrington when they suddenly found themselves in the company of English as well.

Adriana began stammering apologies. "We're sorry, Mr. English. We know we're not invited, but we just couldn't miss this."

"I must speak with you," the big man said gravely. He pulled the three of them aside and walked them to the edge of the group.

The interns exchanged an uneasy glance.

Kaz found his courage. "We have every right to be here. The captain was our friend, too."

English nodded. "*Certainement*, you are right. I owe you this *apologie*, me. You were not to blame for Braden's death. I know this. This is fact."

Dante breathed a sigh of relief. "We thought you were going to kick us out."

"There are many people here you do not know," English told them. "Come. I will introduce."

They were surprised to find that Star was famous among the oil-rig divers. Word had spread that the Antilles platform's hospital was home to a young girl who had gotten the bends while attempting to save Captain Vanover. As Star's friends, Kaz, Adriana, and Dante were famous as well.

"The bends," groaned Henri Roux, Diver 2 on English's team. "I see too many good guys retire into the wheelchair. You make your living at nine hundred feet, sooner or later, the bends gets you, too."

Kaz whistled. "Nine hundred feet! English and I went a third that deep, and we had to carry a hundred pounds of tanks and hang off the line for two hours."

"This is different kind of diving," English explained. "Saturation diving with the hard hat — helmet. Very deep, very dangerous. No tanks. The breathing gas comes from the hose from top-

THE DANGER

side. You decompress in the bell or a chamber, sometimes for many days."

"How far down can you go?" asked Dante in awe.

English shrugged. "Me, the deepest, one thousand three hundred feet. But Tin Man, the one atmosphere suit, it goes deeper. Or the submersible — "

He fell silent. The mention of a submersible brought everyone back to the reason for this gathering.

English clapped two enormous hands together, and the assembly came to order. His voice resounded across the beach.

"We are all the friends of Braden, so you know he was a man of deeds, not words. And if you know me, you see I speak even less. So I just say *merci*.

"Maybe nobody tell you there is a hero in this sad story, a young American girl in the hospital on the main platform. She is sick because she tried to help Braden. If you work on the rig, visit her. She has much courage.

"*Merci* also for the pictures and souvenirs. They will be sent to Braden's family. Tomorrow in Florida they have the funeral. According to Braden's last wishes, it will be a burial at sea."

Kaz's head snapped to attention. "At sea?"

he blurted in dismay. "We almost got ourselves killed getting him *out* of the sea!"

English caught his pop-eyed stare. The Caribbean dive guide and the Canadian hockey player shared a moment of exquisite humor, secure in the knowledge that the man they mourned would have been laughing, too.

CHAPTER TEN

The water was cold. Star could feel it, but the wet suit kept the icy chill at bay. Besides, she was so amped about her first real scuba dive that she wouldn't have noticed a cryogenic freeze.

Her breathing was fast but controlled, the hiss of compressed air louder than she remembered from certification class. It was the Saint Lawrence River in upstate New York — cloudy as pea soup compared with the pristine turquoise of the French West Indies. But back then it was Fantasy Land, a hidden world opening up for Star Ling.

She loved everything about it, and right away. She loved feeling her disability vanish underwater. She loved that there was no law of gravity here, that with the help of her B.C., she could fly.

When the wreck came into view, an excitement took hold that electrified her entire being. She held out her glove to touch a corroded porthole, but the murk made distance difficult to judge. Kicking forward, she reached for the ship's iron skeleton, but the muddy Saint Lawrence held the image just beyond her grasp. . . .

DIVE

* * *

Star shook awake, and the dream popped like a bubble. The first few seconds were like this every morning. Disorientation, followed by depressing reality.

I can't dive. I can't even walk. . . .

She sat up in bed, propping the pillow behind her. In the guest quarters of the humongous platform, she knew, her father was on the phone with the airlines. Ever since his arrival, Dad had been trying to convince her to return to the States for treatment.

She had resisted. "They know more about the bends here than they do at some hospital up in Boston," she had argued. But the fact was, leaving Saint-Luc felt a lot like quitting.

But quitting what? The internship? This had never been a real internship. Cutter and his team were phonies, Gallagher didn't care, and Captain Vanover was gone forever. Kaz, Adriana, and Dante had become real friends, but let's face it — they were just marking time now. It was only early August, yet the summer was over.

And anyway, Star's condition wasn't improving. If the oil-rig doctors couldn't help her, she had to give someone else a chance. Getting back on her feet again — that was the most important thing. Dad was right about that.

THE DANGER

Last night she had given him the okay to book tickets home. It was the smart thing to do. Still . . .

The picture was always the same: a muddy shelf in the ocean's depths, the remains of an ancient vessel. And somewhere in the decayed wreckage —

Don't think about that! she ordered herself. *That makes you no better than Cutter!*

But it wasn't the treasure that tantalized her. It was the *challenge*. Like climbing Everest, or walking on the moon. A goal worthy enough to lend this tragic summer some meaning.

She heard footsteps and looked up to see that she was no longer alone. English stood in the doorway, his expression inscrutable.

He said, "I think maybe today you walk."

Her face flamed red. "What are you telling me? That I'm here because I'm not trying hard enough? I've hit that floor so many times even my bruises have bruises! I *want* to walk — I just can't do it!"

In answer, the huge dive guide snatched her out of bed and carried her, cradled like a baby, into the bustling hallway.

Star flailed her arms against his strength. "Are you crazy? What are you doing?"

He pulled over a rolling cart of instruments and an IV pole on wheels. Then he set her on her feet, her right hand resting on the metal tray, her left grasping the pole.

"I'm gonna *fall* — "

"Alors, fall, mademoiselle." English backed away. "Prove me *stupide*."

Her whole body was trembling. Surgical clamps rattled in the tray. A fluid bag on the pole swung like a pendulum. But Star remained upright.

All at once, her right foot lurched forward. It was only a couple of inches, but it was a step — her first since the accident. Star teetered for an instant and stabilized. Her left foot moved next, followed by the right again. The cart and pole rolled with her as she moved in a slow staccato pace down the hall.

"I'm walking!" she cried in amazement.

It all came apart in an instant. The tray overturned, sending surgical instruments flying. Overbalanced, she pulled the IV pole down on top of herself. English swooped forward and caught her a split second before she would have hit the floor.

In her astonishment, the near miss barely even registered with her.

THE DANGER

"I *walked,*" she whispered in disbelief. "I'm going to walk."

When Adriana saw the message from her brother, she felt guilty immediately. How many times had she sat here in Poseidon's computer lab? Never once had she e-mailed Payton.

Jealousy, she admitted to herself. *He got to go with Uncle Alfie, and I didn't.*

For the past two summers, the Ballantyne kids had been working with their uncle at the British Museum. This year, Alfred Ballantyne had only been allowed one assistant on his Syrian archaeological dig. He had chosen Payton. That was what had brought Adriana to Poseidon in the first place. It was her consolation prize.

Hi, Ade.

Sorry I haven't e-mailed sooner. Uncle Alfie has been keeping me pretty busy, but that's no excuse. Nobody can dig twenty-four hours a day, not even in the desert, where there's nothing else to do.

Two shipwrecks! And I'm stuck here, where it takes eleven hours to brush the sediment off an old jug. I'll bet you're having the time of your life. . . .

She wondered how envious he'd be if he knew that the captain was gone, and Star might never walk again.

Anyway, here's the thing: Uncle Alfie told me about the problem of the bone handle. Why an English artifact on a Spanish galleon? Well, I did a little Web surfing. Guess what? An entire English privateer fleet was caught in the very same hurricane that sank <u>Nuestra Señora</u>. And that's not all.

Check out the Internet address below. Let's see if you come to the same conclusion I did. Then I'll know I'm not crazy. . . .

Adriana felt a twinge of annoyance. *Why does this have to be all about Payton? He's half a world away!*

But she was also intrigued. She maneuvered her mouse to the link and clicked.

The site was British, maintained by the U.K. government's Ministry of Overseas Trade and Commerce. It was a record of English shipping in 1665 — the year of the storm that had sunk *Nuestra Señora*.

According to the register, a privateer fleet had

THE DANGER

indeed sailed from the port of Liverpool in April of that year. Nine of eleven ships survived the Atlantic crossing to carry out a successful attack on the Spanish settlement of Portobelo. The storm struck in September near the infamous Hidden Shoals. There, the English flagship, a barque called the *Griffin*, was lost with all hands.

Adriana leaned back in her chair, frowning. What was Payton getting at? That the deeper shipwreck might be the *Griffin*? And the J.B. handle came from there?

But it didn't make sense. Star had found that artifact in the wreckage of *Nuestra Señora*, up on the reef.

Then it hit her.

The biggest mystery in all this wasn't the handle. It was the question of what had happened to the galleon's huge treasure. All at once, Adriana had the answer.

Privateers were sponsored by governments, but they were basically just pirates. Their mission was to raid, loot, and sink the shipping of their countries' enemies.

If the *Griffin* had met up with *Nuestra Señora de la Luz* on the high seas, it would have attacked. And if they were successful, the privateers would have stolen every single coin on board.

What, then, if the hurricane of 1665 had

destroyed both vessels? One, a Spanish galleon with an empty hold, foundered on the reef. And the other, an English barque, packed to the gunwales with plunder, sank not far away in the deeper water just off the shoal.

"Way to go, Payton!" she cheered aloud.

It was an amazing theory, a *brilliant* theory. It explained everything — why there was no treasure to be found in the *Nuestra Señora* site, and why all evidence pointed to the existence of that treasure in the second, deeper wreck.

It was perfect, Adriana reflected, but it was just a theory. There was still no proof that the other ship really was the *Griffin*, or that she had ever had any contact with *Nuestra Señora*. Adriana felt herself deflating as the elation deserted her. Payton's logic was inspired; it was probably even correct. But it was incomplete.

She was just about to close her computer's Internet browser when she saw it — a small detail on the British Web site.

According to the records, the *Griffin* had been under the command of Captain James Octavius Blade.

James Blade.

J.B.

THE DANGER

CHAPTER ELEVEN

They were a strange procession down the hall of the hospital of the Antilles Oil platform. Star was at the center, taking baby steps, hanging on to the handles of a walker. Kaz, Adriana, and Dante matched her slow pace, leaning into the hushed conversation.

"Captain James Blade," whispered Star. "How cool is that? I wonder what he was like? Maybe some kindly grizzled old sailor, hobbling around on a cane with a bone handle."

"He was a privateer, Star," Adriana reminded her. "They were as bad as pirates, sometimes worse. He may have hobbled, but he wasn't kindly."

"Or he was a maniac with a whip," put in Kaz.

"The point is, he was a rich maniac," said Dante. "Or he would have been if his boat hadn't sunk. Can you imagine that feeling? All your dreams are coming true, and then — "

"I can," Star said huskily. "I'll never dive again."

DIVE

Kaz didn't mean to snap, but the thought of Drew Christiansen set off an avalanche of emotion. "Don't you think that's a little nitpicky? You could be in a wheelchair right now!"

Star's eyes flashed, but she nodded sadly. "I know how lucky I am."

"When are you heading back to the States?" Adriana asked Star.

"Friday morning. Poseidon doesn't want me on the catamaran, so we have to wait for an oil company helicopter to Martinique."

"I can't believe you're leaving," said Kaz.

"My dad can't miss any more work," Star mumbled. "The choppers don't run every day. We've got to grab this one."

They nodded lamely.

"The thing is" — Star looked from face to face — "people like Cutter, treasure hunters, they spend decades searching, all for nothing. But between Dante's eyes, Adriana's smarts, and Kaz's guts, we did the impossible. I mean, we found two needles in the world's biggest haystack. If only I could dive, I'd — "

"You'd what?" challenged Dante. "Swim down to seven hundred feet and bag up a billion dollars? It can't be done."

"It can, you know," Adriana argued. "English

THE DANGER

can do it. The oil-rig divers go that deep all the time. What did they call it?"

"Saturation diving," Kaz supplied. "But that's a big operation — a diving bell, special breathing gas, a support ship — "

"Maybe English and his friends can get the treasure for us," suggested Dante. "One-point-two billion — you can split it a lot of ways and still come out loaded."

"Are you kidding?" exclaimed Star. "English hates treasure hunters. Why do you think he's so mad at Cutter?"

"We're not treasure hunters," Dante argued. "We're just people who happen to know about some treasure. And we may as well get it, because it isn't doing anybody any good sitting around in the mud."

"And the money goes to charity, of course," Adriana added sarcastically.

"What's so bad about wanting money?" Dante shot back. "I don't see your family giving away its millions. Come on, let's just ask the guy."

"It looks like you're going to get your chance," observed Kaz.

They had reached the door of Star's hospital room. There, seated on the edge of the bed, his face unsmiling as always, sat English.

Pushing the walker, Star led the way inside. "Look how fast I'm getting. Think they've got some kind of NASCAR for these things?"

The dive guide got to his feet, towering over the interns. "*Bon*. You are all here. Now you will tell me — on *Deep Scout*, *exactement* what did you find?"

"Sure." Adriana explained their theory of the wrecks of *Nuestra Señora de la Luz* and the *Griffin*, and the vast treasure that lay in the ruins of the second ship. "We can't be positive, but we're ninety-nine percent sure. The J.B. handle proves it. Captain Blade must have lost his walking stick or whip during the battle over *Nuestra Señora*. That's why we found an English artifact in a Spanish galleon."

"One billion American dollars," English repeated gravely.

"One-point-two," amended Dante.

"We didn't think you wanted to know," put in Kaz. "Every time treasure came up, you got mad. What's the big interest now?"

English rested his chin on an enormous fist. "At Poseidon, I see Monsieur Cutter's name on the schedule for use Tin Man. Such equipment is not for working on the reef. I think he tries to find this treasure for himself."

THE DANGER

"But Cutter doesn't even know about the second ship," argued Kaz.

"Perhaps he knows more than you think." English paused reluctantly. "You must not jump on the conclusions. But this thing you should hear: The damage to Deep Scout — this was not the shark attack. It was the sabotage." He explained the tampering he'd observed on the fiberglass plates that covered the sub's temperature probe.

The interns were horrified.

"Cutter!" Adriana exclaimed. "He killed the captain!"

"He could have killed all of us," added Star. "And he nearly put me in a wheelchair."

"I always knew he was a jerk," put in Kaz. "But I never thought he was a murderer."

"I have no proof, me," English said sternly. "When I talk to him, he seems very surprised. Conviction without trial — this is not civilized."

"But how else could he know about the deeper wreck?" Dante persisted.

"We have a saying — on a small island, all the world knows your underwear size. A secret — on Saint-Luc there is no such thing. Me, I do not accuse Monsieur Cutter of murder — yet. Alors, however he learns of this treasure, I think he dives for it Saturday."

"We've got to stop him," Star exclaimed determinedly. "Otherwise we're letting him get rich off the captain's death."

"Stop him," repeated English. "How to do this?"

"By beating him to the treasure," Kaz reasoned. "You know saturation diving; I know where the wreck is. I'll go with you."

"*Absolument*, no."

"I made it to three hundred feet; I can do this, too."

English nodded. "You are brave, monsieur. But you are a boy, and no boy is ready for the sat dive."

Kaz stuck out his chin. "I can dive in a helmet; I can handle an air hose; I can sit in a chamber and decompress — "

"Ah, *oui*," English interrupted. "All these things you can learn. But I ask you this: You have been on my island for more than a month. How many old divers do you see? And the men who yet live, they limp, they ache from the bends, from the arthritis, from the injury. You are children from a wealthy country where danger is for the daredevils. I *must* do this job — I cannot trade the shares on Wall Street. You have the choice. Be smart."

"It's the only way to stop Cutter," argued Kaz. "And you can't do it without me."

THE DANGER

"And me," added Adriana. "This is plundered Spanish treasure in the wreckage of an English privateer! Living history! I have to be a part of it."

"Not me," said Dante. "I'll do what I can; I'll help on the boat. I swore I'd never dive again."

"Bravo," English approved. "Someone has the intelligence."

"It can work," Kaz persisted. "You know it can."

English thought it over. "We will need a ship," he said finally. "A bell. Crew who can be trusted. *Très difficile* — "

"But not impossible," Kaz finished.

The guide took a deep breath. "I will try, me."

Star sat down on the bed. "I can't believe I won't be going down there with you."

"We'll e-mail you," Adriana vowed. "You'll get every detail."

Star regarded the friends who had been closer than family for the past few weeks. "I'll miss you guys," she told them soberly. "I hope we can figure out a way to keep in touch back home."

"If this works, we'll be millionaires," Dante reminded her. "Plane tickets are chicken feed compared to the kind of money we're going to have."

Star choked on the notion that this was really good-bye. "I'd trade it all for the chance to go on one more dive with you."

THE DANGER

08 September 1665

Samuel had tasted battle before, but the long slow approach to the galleon brought out in him a cold, numbing dread he would not have believed possible.

"Why do they not flee?" he whispered to York. "Or fire upon us? Do they not understand our intentions?"

"See how she lists, boy," the barber pointed out. "She's aground. A reef, mayhap. There are treacherous shoals in these seas."

Suddenly, smoke and flame belched from the galleon's gun ports. The roar of the volley echoed across the water. Lethal shot came screaming in on the barque. With a sickening crunch, a cannonball shattered a section in the stern, well above the waterline. The deck collapsed for a few feet around it, sending a handful of seamen sliding into the hold. But most of the projectiles sailed over the Griffin *and disappeared into the water.*

Samuel waited for the barque's guns to respond in kind. Then he noticed that all the gunners were assembled with the attack force, swords and muskets at

DIVE

the ready. Captain Blade had no intention of sinking this galleon, not until her treasure was safely aboard his own vessel.

The Griffin came alongside the Spaniard, and the grappling hooks were airborne. It seemed only a heartbeat later that scores of heavily armed privateers were scrambling up the ropes to the higher decks of the galleon. Steel-helmeted Spanish troops awaited them there. Muskets fired, and sailors with whom Samuel had broken bread for many months dropped lifeless into the sea.

The second wave of privateers caught the defenders reloading. The Englishmen streamed onto the deck. Swords clashed. Men fell.

This was a fight to the death.

It was well known in the New World that a Spanish galleon was an easy target for corsairs and pirates. The ships were overloaded and slow. The sailors were not trained to fight, and the soldiers were underpaid, underfed, and eager to surrender.

No one had shared this information with the gallant crew of a ship called Nuestra Señora de la Luz. The defenders battled like lions, sailors alongside soldiers, and even passengers. The treasure in their hold was the property of His Most Catholic Majesty King Carlos II, and no English pirate was going to get it.

THE DANGER

Samuel had not raised his sword in Portobelo, but he fought today on the deck of this galleon. He did so to preserve his own life. Not a moment went by without razor-sharp steel slicing his way, or a musket ball whizzing past his ear. To the best of his knowledge, he harmed no one. He used his weapon only to ward off the strokes against him.

But that did not keep the blood off him. It was everywhere, spurting and spraying like water. The deck ran with gore, a flood that spilled over the gunwales until the surrounding seas were filled with sharks, driven to frenzy by the taste and smell of a fresh kill.

At the center of the carnage fought Captain James Blade, a broadsword in one hand and his bone-handled whip in the other. This was a man, Samuel knew, who gloried in battle, even enjoyed it. Yet the expression on his face as he flailed about himself was one of naked fear. The possibility of losing this encounter had occurred to him. It was not a thought that had ever crossed his arrogant mind before.

But the privateers had not traversed half a world only to fall short when their prize lay right under the deck planks beneath their feet. When the tide turned in favor of the English, it was through sheer force of stubborn will.

Seven and eighty privateers had gone into battle

just an hour before. Fewer than half that number looked on as the Spanish commander yielded his weapon to Captain Blade, representing the surrender of Nuestra Señora de la Luz.

Blade accepted the sword in a sullen rage. He raised his whip and began to lash the commander, cursing him for putting up such resistance.

A young Spaniard, the first officer, threw himself at Blade, made furious by this dishonorable conduct. He wrested the whip from the corsair's hand and flung it contemptuously overboard.

Samuel never knew what gave him the courage to step forward and try to calm his captain down. "You've won, sir. The treasure is yours. You can buy a thousand whips with gems even bigger than that one."

The words served to placate the captain. But that did not stop him from ordering that every man, woman, and child aboard the galleon be thrown to the sharks.

THE DANGER

CHAPTER TWELVE

English stood in the bow of the *Antilles Adventurer*, appraising the gathering overcast.

Bad weather was coming. That wouldn't affect the divers. At seven hundred feet, the topside conditions might as well have been happening in Paris. But it would certainly be a factor for this sixty-year-old ship. Flat and bargelike, the *Adventurer* wallowed like a garbage scow even in glassy calm. Who knew how she would perform in a storm?

But the boat had two things going for her: She could handle a diving bell and she wasn't on Antilles Oil's work schedule. For an "unofficial" job like this one, English needed a craft that wouldn't be missed.

The six-foot-five figure shuddered slightly in the headwind. Nervousness was not a familiar feeling for Menasce Gérard. He was used to a masterful confidence in his ability to deal with any situation. But treasure hunting did not sit well with him. Nor did the idea of involving his Antilles colleagues in this scheme that could cost

DIVE

them their jobs. But mostly, taking two inexperienced teenagers to seven hundred feet seemed like madness. And yet, this was the only way. So strange, this life!

He could see them now in the late dusk, waiting on the uneven planks of the abandoned marina. Outremont harbor, on Saint-Luc's south coast, had not been used for many years. But it was the perfect place to make the pickup, far from the prying eyes of Cutter or Gallagher or anybody at Antilles Oil.

Since the harbor had not been maintained, English came for them in a dinghy.

Dante stared at the *Adventurer*. "That's the boat?"

"You were expecting the *Queen Mary*, monsieur?" English inquired sarcastically.

The young photographer couldn't take his eyes off the World War II–era ship. "Will it float?"

"Maybe you should dive with us," suggested Kaz. "Then, if it sinks, you'll have time to get out of the way."

Dante bit his lip. "I'll take my chances with the rust bucket."

Once on deck, English introduced the interns to Captain Bourassa and two other oil company seamen. A crew of three was bare minimum to run the *Adventurer*, but English didn't want to risk letting too large a group in on their plan. An oil rig was a gossip mill. People talked. News spread.

English's friend Henri Roux was also there, not to dive, but to handle diving operations from topside.

"Is that everybody?" asked Adriana.

"There is one more — " English began.

"Hi, guys."

From the main companionway, limping only slightly more than usual, emerged Star.

The three stared at her.

"You went home this morning!" exclaimed Dante.

Star grinned. "I *am* home. Wherever the action is — that's home."

"But you can't dive." Kaz turned to English. "You're not going to let her dive."

"Cool your jets, rink rat," Star soothed. "I'm not that nuts. But someone has to look after you guys from topside — make sure Henri doesn't blow the bell full of laughing gas by mistake."

"But what about your dad?" asked Adriana. "Didn't he need to get back to work?"

She shrugged. "I talked him into letting me stay. I'm all checked out of the hospital. The doctor says I'm ninety percent. The rest will come gradually."

"You're doing awesome," Kaz observed.

"But you're still limping," Dante added dubiously.

Star looked exasperated. "Bonehead, I'm still me! The bends doesn't cure cerebral palsy."

English addressed Kaz and Adriana. "It is time to press down to our work depth. This will take more than two hours, so we must begin at once."

The *Adventurer* was equipped with a decompression chamber. English, Kaz, and Adriana were locked inside, and Henri Roux manipulated the controls, gradually increasing the pressure. By the time the bell reached the wreck site at 703 feet, the three divers had to be used to the crushing weight of twenty-two atmospheres.

There was an insistent hiss as gas flooded the chamber. Adriana's ears hurt almost immediately. She squeezed her nose and blew out. There was a squeal as the pressure equalized. She would be doing this for the next two and a half hours.

The things I put up with for archaeology!

Star's face appeared at the chamber's window. "Ears pop yet?" she asked over the intercom.

THE DANGER

"It feels like somebody set off a cherry bomb in my skull," Adriana replied in a squeaky tone. Saturation divers breathed a mixture of helium and oxygen called heliox. It made you sound like a Munchkin.

Kaz adapted his high-pitched voice into a perfect Bart Simpson impression that had Adriana howling with laughter. Outside the chamber, Star and Dante were practically rolling on the deck.

Even English's baritone was shrill and distorted. "Monsieur Simpson, he is a diver?"

Dante was nearly hysterical. "He's a cartoon on TV!"

"Ah, yes. Your American television." English displayed no hint of a smile. "Amuse yourselves now. On the bottom, there is no laughing, only danger."

"We'll stick to you like glue," Kaz promised.

"That is no help at seven hundred feet. With the backup tank, you breathe maybe three minutes. Ascent, this means only death from the bends. *Alors*, you have one choice — the perfection."

"Aw, lighten up, Mr. English," Dante wheedled. "We're all going to be rich. What are you going to do with your share of the money?"

"I will do nothing," English replied readily.

"Come on," chided Kaz. "You could buy a nice car."

"I do not drive."

"A big house?" prompted Dante. "On the water, maybe?"

"Everything I need, I have."

"What about travel?" suggested Adriana. "Wouldn't it be great to see the world?"

English gave them a disinterested shrug. "Where do people go for vacation? The islands. Me, I am already here. But," he added, "the first money from any treasure will repay Antilles Oil for use their equipment. Another share should go to Braden's family, no?"

Star nodded. "And Iggy Ocasek. He helped us find the deeper wreck."

"I'm going to give some of my share to this guy back home," said Kaz. "A hockey player. He's got — medical bills."

"I haven't thought about what I'm going to do with my share," Adriana told them. "Donate it to charity, I guess."

Dante rolled his eyes. "Yeah, me, too. I'm donating mine to the Dante Foundation."

"For now, there is no money, only talk," English said sharply. "Remember this — gold is valuable because it is hard to get, not easy. And harder still to keep."

THE DANGER

It took two hours for the slow-moving ship to reach the coordinates of the wreck site at the edge of the Hidden Shoals. By this time, the three divers were sweltering in their watertight "dry" suits, waiting to transfer to the bell. The bell was pressurized and docked with the chamber by means of an airtight tunnel. The three crawled through into the cramped space that would be their home for the operation to come. They carried their Ratcliff diving helmets — Rat Hats.

The bell was dark and damp, and smelled like a locker room after the big game — the odor of physical labor, bodies, perspiration. The walls were curved, with view ports barely the size of CDs. There was no floor that Adriana could see. They settled themselves uncomfortably on endless piles of coiled umbilical lines. English pulled the hatch shut with a muffled thud.

According to the gauge, the pressure was already equivalent to a depth of 660 feet. *It's happening*, Adriana thought to herself. *We're really going to do this.*

Henri's voice came through the interphone box. "Can you read me in the pot?"

They could hear Dante in the background. "Hey, what does this switch do?"

A quick, sharp slap was clearly broadcast over the hookup, followed by Star's voice: "Cut it out, Dante!"

"Topside, we read you," English reported with a sigh. He added, "Please do not let that annoying child touch anything."

The *Adventurer's* powerful spotlights came on suddenly, capturing the bell like a stage performer. Inside, tubes of light leaped from the round ports. There were a few minutes of equipment checks, followed by the roar of the winch. The bell lifted shakily off the deck.

"Stand by in the pot." There was a jolt, and they were in the water, sinking through deepening shades of blue.

Adriana was amazed at how quickly the sweaty heat deserted them. She hugged her bulky dry suit. "Is anybody else freezing?"

English nodded. "This is normal. The helium — it makes you lose warmth faster than air."

As they descended quickly, English checked the umbilicals, which were really several different lines, taped together like bundles of spaghetti strands — breathing supply, phone cable, safety rope. There was also an extra hose so that hot water could be pumped through a system of tubing that crisscrossed the fabric of their dry suits.

THE DANGER

This would provide warmth against the icy chill of the deep sea.

All at once, English announced, "We are arrived."

"So fast?" blurted Adriana.

Seven hundred feet may be an alien world, she reminded herself. *But the actual distance to the surface is a little more than an eighth of a mile.*

English pushed aside cables, welding torches, and a few plastic sandwich bags of high-energy snacks to clear the bell's work-lock beneath their feet. He opened the double hatch to reveal water the color of intergalactic space. The blackness washed upward at first, as if it were about to flood the bell. But then the pressure equalized, halting the ocean's advance.

English helped Kaz and Adriana seal the big fiberglass helmets to their suits before donning his own. Suddenly top-heavy, Adriana overbalanced and conked her Rat Hat into the wall of the bell. "I'm okay," she muttered, recovering. The heliox tasted metallic in the close quarters of the headgear.

"Topside," English reported. "Hats on."

Adriana heard Henri's voice coming from a small speaker by her ear. "Comm. check. Everybody reads me, yes?"

"Loud and clear," she replied into the helmet's built-in microphone.

"Me, too," said Kaz. "Man, this sure beats scuba!"

The three divers stepped into flippers. "Locking out," reported English.

And they dropped into the molasses-dark.

THE DANGER

CHAPTER THIRTEEN

The *Adventurer's* topside dive station was an odd place for a communications center. The roar from the compressors in the gas shack made it nearly impossible to hear. But Henri, Star, and Dante bent over the console, listening to every word from seven hundred feet.

The divers had been out of the bell for an hour already, and they still hadn't been able to locate the wreck site.

"Don't you remember?" Star said urgently into the microphone. "There was junk scattered all the way down the slope, but the main shipwreck landed on kind of a shelf."

"Well, we found the slope," Adriana reported, her voice distorted by helium. "We just can't find the shelf."

"What do you mean, you can't find it?" Dante demanded. "The coordinates are right, the depth is right — "

"It's a little dark down here, Dante," Kaz squeaked, annoyed. "I can't even see Adriana and English unless there's a light shining right on them."

DIVE

"But it's there," insisted Dante. "It has to be!"

"Enough!" English's voice was stern, despite the high tone. "This is not the time for the debate. We search. And if we find nothing, we go home. *Alors*, this is all we can do."

"But Cutter's getting Tin Man tomorrow," Dante reminded them. "That's in seven hours!"

Star pulled him aside. "Let them work in peace," she said in a low voice.

"That's in seven hours!"

"They *know* that," she assured him. "But scaring them isn't going to help them find anything — "

Dante wheeled away from her and faced Henri. "I want to go down there."

The dive master frowned. "English says — "

Dante cut him off. "I see things that other people don't. I'll find that wreck site."

"No way," said Star. "You don't take a guy who isn't comfortable diving and send him to seven hundred feet."

"You do if he's the only guy who can find a billion dollars!"

"It's too late anyway," Star told him. "We've only got one bell."

Dante pointed to the lift basket that hung on the smaller winch next to the crane that controlled the bell. It was to be lowered to the wreck site to be filled with treasure. "It's going down anyway.

THE DANGER

What's the difference if I hitch a ride on it?"

"You must descend very slow," Henri said thoughtfully. "Two hours, maybe more."

"Yeah, right," Star snorted at Dante. "You're afraid to scuba dive, but you can sit in a cage for two hours watching the water around you turn black. You won't make it, Dante. You'll freak out and do something stupid. And then you'll get yourself killed for sure."

"You think I want this?" Dante snapped. "You think I want to risk my life and spend four days decompressing? I'd be thrilled to stay topside while everybody else dives. But I'm the guy who can get it done. End of story."

Henri took Dante to get suited up while Star reported the change of plan to the divers.

"I forbid this!" exclaimed English.

The three interns told him about Dante's color blindness. "He only sees in black and white," Adriana explained, "but he can spot shadings underwater that nobody else can. If anybody can find that wreck, it's him."

English was still skeptical. "And the boy, he is not frightened?"

"He's terrified," Star admitted. "But I've never seen him so determined." She sighed. "I wish I was going down with him."

"You must be more careful what you wish for, mademoiselle," the guide told her solemnly.

Dante clung to the lift basket to keep himself from shaking. Just gearing up for this dive was enough to bring on panic. The bulky dry suit constricted him as if he had been mummified, and the Rat Hat reminded him of a medieval torture device. Dangling at the end of the umbilical, he felt like a worm on a hook.

It was not a smooth and even descent. Instead, he was being ratcheted to the depths in a series of ten-foot drops. In between, the basket would stop for ninety maddening seconds. This allowed him to adjust to the pressure, until it was time for the winch to jerk him downward once more. It was frustratingly slow, but that wasn't the worst part. Waiting for the halted basket to move again was the worst kind of mental strain.

At least he wasn't bored. Thanks to the Rat Hat's comm. system, he could listen in on the other divers as they searched. Henri gave him constant updates on his breathing mix, which changed the deeper Dante got. And Star kept him busy by asking, "How's it going down there?" with every grinding of the winch.

"Oh, great," Dante muttered, his voice

THE DANGER

Mickey Moused by heliox. "An electric eel just wrapped around my helmet, and now I'm picking up Radio Australia."

Many fathoms below, Kaz chuckled. "Good one."

"Can it, rink rat," Star grumbled. "I'm just trying to make sure the guy's okay."

"Of course I'm not okay," Dante told her. "I'm diving, aren't I?"

The blackness began around three hundred feet and, by five hundred, Dante felt as if he were suspended in ink. His hand torch provided some visibility. But the cone of light it squeezed into the void seemed to shrink the deeper he got.

It's like being blind. Did he really have a prayer of finding the wreck site in this nothingness?

He spotted the floodlights on the bell long before the other divers were able to see him. By this time, he had been in the lift basket so long that he wasn't sure his stiff body could even move. But it did and, at 680 feet, he allowed Kaz and English to haul him out of the tight mesh.

English carefully detached Dante from the topside hoses and tethered him to an umbilical from the bell. This would enable him to return to the surface in the pot with the other divers when the mission was over.

Okay, time to get rich, Dante thought.

The ship they believed to be the *Griffin* had rained debris all the way down the slant, before coming to rest on a tilted ledge at seven hundred feet.

Find the ledge and you've found the treasure.

He joined the search, tracking back and forth over the featureless slope. He could not have imagined such terrible visibility.

You could swim past a five-star hotel if it wasn't right in your light.

"What do you think?" asked Kaz. "Are you seeing any more than the rest of us?"

"Black is black," Dante replied gloomily. "In color or black and white."

In fact, he was probably seeing less than anybody. His glasses were slowly but steadily fogging inside the Rat Hat. He squinted in concentration, focusing on the dim oval his torch projected onto the muddy grade. Another hour passed. It seemed like a week.

As he panned the endless parade of sand and muck, a round object raced through his field of vision. The others might easily have missed it. But in the gray-on-gray world of Dante's color blindness, shape and texture were everything. He backtracked and picked up the circular form.

THE DANGER

It was a metal plate, pewter probably. *Definitely* very old.

Heart pounding, he shined his light to the left. There was nothing but the underwater moonscape of the seafloor.

Huh? But where's the —

Beginning to despair, he turned to the right.

The wreck of a seventeenth-century ship winked into ghostly existence in the murky beam.

He tried to call "Guys!" but he began to cough, choking on his own excitement.

"Dante!" cried Kaz. "You okay?"

"I found it!" Dante rasped through hacking and helium. "The shelf! The wreck!"

"Don't move," ordered English. "We come to you."

"Okay." Dante couldn't take his eyes off the remains of the old vessel. It was almost as if he expected the site to disappear the instant he looked away. Dishware, bottles, muskets, and helmets littered the angled plateau, along with larger items like anchors and cannon barrels. Ballast stones were everywhere. Half-buried timbers poked out from the bottom silt, all that was left of the spine of the wooden craft.

Now the hard part, he thought to himself. *Finding treasure in this mess.*

He dropped to his knees, digging an arm experimentally into the soft muck of the shelf. He cleared it away, and aimed his light into the hole. An unmistakable yellow glow shone back at him.

Dante Lewis was staring into a vast pile of gold bars.

CHAPTER FOURTEEN

It was well after midnight, but the quiet of Côte Saint-Luc harbor was shattered by the rattle and roar of the winch of the R/V *Ponce de Léon*. The thousand-pound piece of equipment being lowered to the research deck was a sight straight out of *Star Wars*. It looked like an eight-foot-tall metal-plated robot, with side-mounted thrusters and mechanical claw hands.

It was Tin Man, Poseidon's one-atmosphere suit, capable of taking a diver to a depth of two thousand feet or more. Tad Cutter had signed it out at exactly 12:01 A.M. Saturday morning.

"I don't see why this couldn't wait until we all got some sleep," yawned Chris Reardon, guiding the huge suit into place for the ride to the wreck site. With a grunt, he added, "This thing weighs a ton."

"Half a ton," corrected Marina.

"We've only got it for a day, and I'm not taking the chance of coming up empty," Cutter explained. "The kids are onto us. English is suspicious. It's time to claim the treasure before some-

DIVE

body beats us to it." He signaled to Captain Bill Hamilton in the wheelhouse. "Ready to go!"

Thunder rumbled as the *Ponce de Léon* picked its way out of the harbor, and headed into open water. Distant lightning illuminated the overcast at the horizon.

They had not yet made it to the wreck site when Captain Hamilton cut lights and power, and called his three passengers to the bridge. "There's a ship ahead," he informed them. "Looks like an old clunker. The oil company has a few still active."

"Did they see us?" asked Marina.

"I don't think so," replied Hamilton. "I went dark as soon as they came up on radar. They wouldn't have visual contact yet."

"You did the right thing," Cutter approved. "Let's stay here and play dead until they pass by."

"They won't pass by," Hamilton told him. "They're anchored. In just about the exact coordinates we're looking for."

"No way," said Reardon in consternation. "There's no oil on this side of the island."

"English!" breathed Marina. "The kids must have told him where the treasure is. And he's put together a team of sat divers to go after it!"

THE DANGER

Cutter let fly a string of curses. "Those guys are pros! If there's anything to find, they'll find it."

"It doesn't matter," countered Marina. "If they're diving sat, they've got days of decompression ahead of them. All we have to do is go down in Tin Man and get one piece of treasure. Then the International Maritime Commission declares the wreck is ours. It won't make any difference if English and his pals pick that ship dry. They'll just be saving us the trouble."

Seven hundred feet below, the interns shrieked, sang, and sobbed out their celebration. They had been belittled, ignored, and deceived. Now, finally, they had their reward — gold, not at the end of the rainbow, but at the bottom of the sea.

Gold, gold, and more gold!

"What's going on down there?" cried Star. "Are you guys all right?"

"You — you won't believe it — " babbled Dante. "You gotta see it — "

"Will somebody tell me what's going on?!"

Kaz provided the answer. "Dante hit Fort Knox."

And the party spread to sea level.

For three and a half centuries, the ocean had concealed this prize from armies of treasure hunters, oceanographic experts, and professional divers. Yet four kids on a summer program had managed to unravel the puzzle — with a little help from a West Indian Frenchman named English. And Captain Vanover, of course.

The captain. It was the only melancholy note in this exultant symphony. Braden Vanover should have been here to share this triumph.

Now came the business of recovering the spectacular find. Captain Bourassa repositioned the ship so that the bell and lift basket were directly over the shelf. The divers changed from flippers to weighted boots. Swimming was no longer required. A vast fortune was buried right here. It was simply a matter of digging it up.

After eluding human hands for so long, the treasure of *Nuestra Señora de la Luz* seemed to give itself up in a single glittering moment. Kaz and Dante pulled hundreds of gold coins and ingots of all shapes and sizes out of the seabed. English yanked on what looked like a chain, only to come up with a rope of gold nine feet long. There turned out to be dozens of these. Beneath them, Adriana uncovered strings of pearls, and necklaces decorated with rubies, emeralds, and sapphires that made her mother's expensive jewelry seem like dime-store junk.

Gold and gems were easy to spot, but silver was another matter. Silver oxidizes over centuries

THE DANGER

underwater, so the valuable Spanish pieces of eight were now flat black discs. They littered the bottom like gravel.

"We need a shovel," panted Kaz. He had lost count of his armloads.

"Or a bulldozer," Dante added exultantly.

Even English had trouble keeping the smile off his normally sour face. "Monsieur Cutter, he will — how do you say — have the cow."

"I'm having one myself," put in Adriana. "And my uncle — "

"I wonder how long it'll take to get the whole one-point-two billion," mused Dante.

"Yesterday you refused to dive," put in Kaz. "Now you want to stay here forever?"

"Dante," Adriana explained patiently, "the treasure of a Spanish galleon would fill that basket fifty times."

Star cut in from topside. "I want you guys to come up as soon as you start to feel bushed. Don't try to be heroes. Remember, it only takes one piece to put a claim on the whole wreck."

It was unreal — a scene straight out of some swashbuckling adventure story. The very mud under their boots glittered from the pounds of gold dust that had been dispersed by the whirlpool of the sinking ship. It seemed as if every square foot of bottom silt held something of great value —

gemstone-encrusted medallions and crucifixes, silver cups and plates, solid-gold candlesticks, even hatbands and collars made with braided gold. Dante was disappointed when the jewelry box he pulled out of the mud turned out to be bronze. Then he opened the lid and realized that the thing was packed to the top with huge pearls.

Adriana was on her knees, gathering loose gems, when she spied a strange shape half-buried in the sand. In surprise, she realized that it was wood — blackened and made rock-hard by the centuries at depth and pressure. Intrigued, she played her light over the carved contours and curves. The artifact had been broken on one end. She frowned. Why did the jagged angles of the crack seem so familiar?

When the answer came to her, she nearly cried out in amazement. This, she realized, was the most amazing find of all. Her heavy boots sinking in the mud, she carried the piece to the lift basket and dropped it on top of the growing mountain of riches.

When she looked up again, she saw the intruder.

It was moving slowly but steadily toward them, emerging from the darkness into the cocoon of light cast by the bell. She stared at the armored contraption that was cruising in, powered

THE DANGER

by twin thrusters. For a moment, she toyed with the possibility that the depth had driven her to hallucinations. This looked like something from outer space!

And then she recognized it. Tin Man, Poseidon's one-atmosphere suit, sailing through the water like a humanoid submarine. Tad Cutter!

She tried to call out a warning to the others, but she couldn't make her mouth work. How would the treasure hunter react to the sight of the wealth of *Nuestra Señora* being loaded up by someone else? He had already committed one murder out of greed.

The aluminum-plated suit cruised past the wreck site to the lift basket, not ten feet from Adriana. A bulky arm reached into the cage, and a mechanical claw hand closed on a small gold bar.

Despite her terror, the theft puzzled Adriana. Sure, the ingot was valuable. But it was small change compared to the fortune in the basket.

Star's words came back to her: "It only takes one piece of treasure to put a claim on the whole wreck."

We could lose it all if we don't stop him!

Finding her helium-squeaky voice at last, she rasped a warning to the others: "Cutter!"

But Tin Man was retreating from her, gliding

steadily away from the shelf toward the cover of the ocean's cloak.

Kicking off his heavy boots for more speed, English dove for the suit like a linebacker. The comm. system clearly broadcast his "oof!" as he made contact. He hung on, struggling to lock onto the metallic shell.

"What's going on?" came Star's query from topside. "Did somebody say *Cutter?*"

Adriana didn't answer. She was already running in an awkward slow-motion gait, determined to help English, who was being tossed around like a rag doll by Tin Man's hydraulics. The six-foot-five guide looked like a child next to the half-ton suit.

"Help, you guys!" Adriana cried, launching herself into the battle. She grabbed on to the suit's huge leg and hung on for dear life.

"The bell!" English ordered in a strained voice. "Go to the bell! *Vite!*"

"No!" Adriana shrieked. But his logic was clear. If English couldn't handle this sea monster, what hope did a thirteen-year-old girl have?

But I can't just leave him to fight alone!

With a superhuman effort, she scrambled up the fortresslike body. Now she could see Kaz and Dante plodding across the wreck site toward them, battling against the weights on their boots.

THE DANGER

Henri was yelling in French over the comm. system, adding volume every time he got no answer.

English's grunts were directed only at the interns. "Stay away! . . . go back! . . . the bell! . . ."

Straining, Adriana pulled herself up higher, until she was looking into Tin Man's Plexiglas bubble.

A yelp of surprise escaped her.

It was not Tad Cutter in there, attempting to steal their find. The face inside the one-atmosphere suit belonged to Marina Kappas.

CHAPTER FIFTEEN

Aboard the RV *Ponce de Léon*, Chris Reardon crouched over the communications panel, flipping switches and pressing buttons.

"Come in, Marina! Do you read me?"

Cutter sat beside him at a small fold-down table, pounding the keyboard of Marina's laptop. She had been trained on one-atmosphere suits in California. The technical manuals were saved on her computer.

"I found everything about Tin Man except where to oil the hinges," he complained, opening files at light speed. "As far as I can see, we're doing everything right."

"Then she just stopped talking," Reardon concluded. "I hope she's all right." He turned back to the microphone. "Say something, Marina. We're getting nervous here."

Lightning flashed, followed by a crash of thunder. "Weather's getting close," Cutter observed. "Maybe that's the problem."

Reardon frowned. "We won't stay hidden forever. The storm will light us up."

THE DANGER

Cutter said nothing. He was staring in wide-eyed horror at the computer screen.

Reardon glanced at him. "What?"

In answer, Cutter swiveled the laptop so that his companion could see the display. It was a schematic diagram of a deep-ocean submersible.

"That's not Tin Man," Reardon pointed out.

"It's *Deep Scout!*" Cutter exclaimed.

Reardon was confused. "Why would she need the specs of the sub? We never used it."

"The accident!" Cutter's voice was trembling. "English said it was sabotage! I thought he was crazy. But look." He paged down.

Now the screen showed a close-up of the fiberglass plates that protected the temperature probe in the belly of the sub. "Those are the exact same plates that failed on *Deep Scout.*"

"So?" Light dawned on Reardon. "You're not saying that *Marina* rigged the sub? My God, Braden Vanover *died* in that accident!"

Cutter looked pasty in the artificial light. "A submersible must have ten thousand parts. Marina has the drawing for only one of them. It can't be a coincidence!"

"Don't you understand what this means? She's a *murderer!*"

Cutter was in a full panic. "And she's down

where there could be divers in the water! Maybe *that's* why she isn't answering us. Who knows what she could be doing?"

Reardon was shaking now. "Tad, I'm just in this for the money. No one said anybody was going to get killed!"

The decision tore Tad Cutter in two. A man was dead already, and more lives could be at stake. But if he warned the oil company's ship, he would be giving up any chance whatsoever to recover the treasure of *Nuestra Señora de la Luz,* an operation he'd been planning for years.

He hesitated. A billion dollars. A life's dream.

And then he pressed the intercom to Captain Hamilton in the wheelhouse. "Bill, hail the other boat." He sighed. "And you'd better forget about buying that Ferrari."

Far below, all four hard-hat divers were clamped onto Tin Man's husk in a desperate attempt to wrest the gold bar from the iron grip of its mechanical claw.

Star's agitated voice burst into their helmets. "What's going on down there? Has it got anything to do with Marina?"

"She's got some gold!" wheezed Dante. "And she's wearing a U-boat!"

THE DANGER

"It's a one-atmosphere suit," Star said urgently. "Cutter just called to warn us. He thinks she's dangerous!"

Tin Man's flailing arm dealt a tremendous blow to Kaz's Rat Hat. The helmet protected him, but the collision with a thousand-pound piece of equipment knocked him senseless. The force of it sent him tumbling head over heels through the water, his umbilical trailing behind him. The silt cushioned his landing, but he felt nothing anyway. Everything went dark.

English pulled a long knife from a scabbard on his weight belt.

Adriana stared in disbelief. "That can't break through metal!" she gasped.

But that was not the dive guide's plan. Instead, he jammed the blade into the grip of Tin Man's mechanical claw. Using the weapon as a lever, he pried with all his might. The steel snapped, but the gold bar popped free. English dropped the hilt and snatched it up.

"Topside!" he barked. "Raise the basket!"

"Is everybody okay?" pleaded Star.

"The basket!!"

The cage began to rise silently, bearing its treasure trove toward the surface.

The sight of this mountain of wealth being lifted out of her grasp drove Marina to rage. Both claws swiped at English, scissoring through the water. One of the pincers caught the shoulder of his dry suit, cutting through the heavy material like it was newsprint. Frigid water flooded the dive guide's body.

"Back to the bell!" he ordered, shivering.

This time, Adriana and Dante didn't argue. They let go of Tin Man, sinking to the shelf.

Left alone against the armored suit, English was at a serious disadvantage. Marina smacked him across the chest with Tin Man's elbow joint. Then the claw reached for his Rat Hat.

Desperately, he ducked. It was the wrong thing to do. The pincers sliced through his umbilical lines, severing them all. A cascade of bubbles erupted from the heliox hose.

Knowing he only had a few lungfuls of gas left in his helmet, English exploded into action. Bracing against Tin Man's massive shoulders, he vaulted up to the suit's lighting array. He reared back the gold ingot and, one by one, smashed the three floodlights.

Marina grabbed for him again. English switched off his own light, disappearing into the dark ocean before her. She could see only the blinding illumination of the bell. More than a few feet away from that, everything faded to black.

Holding his breath as the Rat Hat filled with

THE DANGER

water, English kicked for the bell. Adriana and Dante were right below the hatch, still plodding along in their boots. He streaked past them and burst through the open work-lock. One big breath, and he was down again, pulling them inside to safety.

The broad flat deck of the *Adventurer* tossed in the worsening storm. Heavy rain pelted the comm. station and gas shack. Forks of lightning carved up the angry sky. Thunder drowned out the roar of the winch as it labored to haul the lift basket full of treasure to the surface.

Star and Henri hung on to bulkheads, still barking frantic queries down to the divers. So far, their only responses had been terrifying sounds of struggle and violence.

And then English's voice: "You are all right? You are unhurt?"

Henri let out a whoop. "They are back in the pot!" He leaned into the microphone. "This is topside. We raise the bell, yes?"

"No!" shrilled Adriana. "We're missing Kaz!"

"Missing?" Star echoed. "What do you mean, missing?"

"Marina hit him in the head!" Dante croaked. "He isn't answering us! I think he's unconscious!"

"I will find him, me," English vowed.

"We're going with you," exclaimed Adriana.

"No!" snapped the guide. "If you move from this bell, I will kill you myself! *Entendu?*"

All at once, the boiling clouds lit up like day. Lightning hit with a shattering roar, turning the *Adventurer*'s antenna into a pyrotechnics display. The thunderclap was instant, coming with a shower of sparks. The strike traveled through every electrical system on the ship, frying lights, radar, sonar, comm. panels, and appliances. Even the microphone blew up in Star's hand.

The crane that controlled the basket of treasure ground to a halt. So did the heliox compressors.

Henri was nothing short of frantic. "The backup generator!" With the compressors dead, there was no breathing gas going down to the divers.

Grabbing flashlights from a rack of emergency equipment, he and Star raced into the gas shack. The backup generator looked like an ancient car engine, about the size of a dishwasher.

Star stared at it in dismay. "Their lives depend on *that?*"

Henri pulled out the choke handle and yanked a cord similar to the starter on a lawn-

THE DANGER

mower. Like an old man with a chronic cough, the contraption sputtered twice, and then put-putted to life in a cloud of burning oil.

They held their breath. A few seconds later, the compressors clamored back into operation.

Star let out a long sigh of relief. "Now how do we get communication back?"

"With a miracle only," the dive master replied sadly. "The wires, they are — how do you say in America — toast. *Fini.*"

Star's eyes were haunted. There was no way of knowing what was going on below.

CHAPTER SIXTEEN

"Say something, Marina. We know you can hear us!"

The weary voice of Tad Cutter echoed inside the sealed environment of the one-atmosphere suit. Marina continued to ignore him, scanning the darkness for a sign of the missing intern. What was there to talk about, after all?

She wondered how her two partners had learned that she had been behind the sabotage of *Deep Scout*. It didn't matter. They had already ratted her out to English's crew. Which meant that the partnership was at an end.

Unease began to seep into her usual confidence. This was not going the way she'd planned it. She's lost the gold bar, the proof of their find. The lift basket was out of reach, and English had destroyed Tin Man's lighting array. Now she was working blind.

"Give it up," Cutter pleaded. "You've already gotten us mixed up in one murder."

The words were out before she could hold them back. "Do you really believe I thought somebody was going to get killed? All I wanted to do was flub the dive!"

"But why?"

"Because we were *losing!*" she raged. "We're still losing! To a bunch of snot-nosed kids!"

"It's just money, Marina. It isn't worth people's lives."

"It's a billion dollars!" she shot back. "It's worth anything!"

Inside the armored suit, she stiffened like a pointer. There in the black void of the deep ocean, a faint light flickered.

The missing intern.

The plan came together in her mind. She would trade this teenager for the bar of gold English had taken from her. It wasn't too late! She could claim this treasure yet.

As her finger operated the miniature controls for Tin Man's thrusters, Tad was still raving about how it was all over, and she should give herself up.

She cut the comm. link. He had nothing to say anymore that would interest her.

Kaz came awake, shivering with cold. He remembered the altercation with Marina in Tin Man, recalled clearly the savage blow she had dealt him.

But why am I freezing to death?

He wriggled within his dry suit and felt no warmth from the hot-water tubes that crisscrossed the fabric. The hit he had taken must have damaged the heating hose in his umbilical.

What about communications?

"English?" he ventured. "Guys? Topside?"

No answer. Comms. were out, too.

With awareness, fear also returned. He could see nothing in the inky sea except for the bell, hanging in a corona of light. There was no sign of the others. Were they waiting in the pot or out looking for him? And Marina? Had she gotten away with that gold bar?

He panned the sea with his light, but the small torch barely made a dent in the blackness.

Then the glowing bell disappeared, and the huge dark shape of Tin Man loomed over him, claws reaching.

He fled right out of his weighted boots, leaving them rooted in the mud. As he swam, he realized with a sinking heart that he would never outrun Tin Man's thrusters. He needed a hiding place. But where?

He was nearing the point where the shelf ended, and the ocean floor sheered up into the slope that marked the edge of the Hidden Shoals. He was just about to douse his torch and try to

THE DANGER

lose himself in the darkness when he spotted it — a large gash in the joint formed where the ledge met the grade. Switching off his light, he kicked his way inside.

The darkness was total, almost choking him. The terror of the moment was truly paralyzing, for he knew that he would never see Tin Man's powerful pincers. He would not realize the hunter was near until he was already taken.

There he cowered, hugging the mud bottom for any trace of warmth, listening to the chattering of his teeth and — another sound. Was it the whir of Tin Man's thrusters? No, it didn't seem to be mechanical. It was more like a low, steady gurgling.

What could it be? There's nothing down here!

After what seemed like an eternity, he worked up his courage and switched on his torch.

What he saw turned his limbs to lead and brought him to his knees in the sand. The opening in the sea floor formed a large grotto with a silt bottom and a rocky ceiling. The gurgling turned out to be an underwater vent that sent an explosion of bubbles coursing through the cave. But it was not this natural phenomenon that churned his stomach to Cool Whip.

It was the sharks.

CHAPTER SEVENTEEN

Kaz knew a lot about sharks. Their cold black eyes, torpedolike bodies, and gaping jaws full of razor-sharp teeth had haunted his dreams as far back as he could remember. His phobia had been cranked higher and tighter over the years by a personal library of books about the notorious sea predators, constantly read and reread. Kaz knew, for example, that all sharks had to swim to survive. There was only one exception to this rule: when an underwater vent created a stream of bubbles that could aerate the gills of a "sleeping" shark.

There were six animals assembled along the path of bubbles, hanging perfectly still. Five were blue sharks, ranging in length from four to seven feet. It was the remaining one, the biggest, that drew his eyes and filled him with unspeakable horror.

Clarence, the eighteen-foot tiger shark of local legend. Two tons of destructive power, with a mouth large enough to swallow a fourteen-year-old hockey player whole.

For weeks, the interns had pondered what

THE DANGER

had kept this monster in the waters around Saint-Luc while other tigers wandered the oceans. They had questioned what had lured it from the abundant food of the reef down to the empty depths. At last, the mystery was revealed — this vent, this special place.

Yet there was no moment of enlightenment, no finger-snapping understanding. Kaz realized too late that his light had been shining directly into Clarence's unhooded black eye. The crescent tail moved first — just a twitch. That muscle contraction traveled all the way along the eighteen-foot body. The head swung toward him, giving Kaz a view past the forest of serrated teeth, clear into the predator's cavernous gullet.

He felt his grip on reality starting to slip away. In that instant, he forgot Marina in the one-atmosphere suit, and a billion dollars in treasure. His universe became, quite simply, the nine feet of water separating him from his ultimate nightmare — to be ripped apart and devoured as prey.

And then the mouth opened like a garage door as the huge shark attacked.

Kaz did the only thing he could think of. He tried to insert himself into the floor of the grotto. To his immense shock and relief, there was a space for him, a fine groove in the rock beneath the silt. He wriggled into it, thinking small.

The flat snout slammed against his hip. Impact. Pain. He waited for the crushing bite, the tearing wrench of the monster's jaws.

It didn't come. The sawing teeth could not reach him! He switched off his light and huddled in the tiny niche, smothering in his own bottomless dread.

Go away. His mind could conjure up no other words. Go away, go away, go away. Shaking with hypothermia and fear, he clung to his hiding place with mindless intensity. He didn't think about the others, the bell, rescue. Here was safe; here was good. That was all that mattered.

Time passed. Seconds? Minutes? There was no clock on his terror.

It happened without warning, not a hiss, not a click. The supply of breathing gas to his Rat Hat simply stopped.

No!!!

His first notion was completely irrational — that Clarence, unable to pry him from the gash in the rock, had bitten through his umbilical in order to draw him out.

Impossible! A shark's too dumb to come up with a plan like that!

THE DANGER

Amazingly, the crisis forced his unreasoning panic to the edges, leaving room for rational thought. This was a diving problem. He was trained for that. Kaz carried a backup tank of heliox for emergencies just like this one. But he would be unable to reach it without coming out of the crack.

With a silent prayer, he switched on his torch. The blue sharks still slumbered in the bubble stream. There was no sign of Clarence.

Water began to dribble into the Rat Hat as the gas remaining in the hose was used up.

Holding his breath, he climbed out of his hiding place and snapped the hose from the bailout bottle to the intake valve on his helmet.

The metallic tang of heliox. But for how long? At this depth and pressure, gas was gone in the blink of an eye. This tank might last an hour on the surface. But here at twenty-two atmospheres — he did the math — less than three minutes. If he couldn't get to the bell in that time, he would die.

He paddled out of the cave, legs kicking madly. He would have given anything for a pair of flippers. But there was no time to think about that now.

There it was — the bell, glowing like a distant diamond off to his left. He pointed the Rat Hat in its direction and kicked for his life. Maximum speed on minimum heliox — that's what he needed.

He was breathing too fast, he was sure.

But I can make it!

A dark shape moved in front of the gleaming sphere of the bell. Kaz's hope disintegrated in a puff of precious gas. Tin Man! Marina Kappas stood in the sand of the shelf between him and his goal.

It all came clear. Marina had cut his umbilical to bring him out of hiding. And now he was swimming right into the clutches of Tin Man's powerful hydraulics. It was virtual suicide. But he had no choice. He was already running low on gas. All he could do was make for the bell.

And pray.

Another half breath, and the tank went bone-dry. Kaz swallowed hard and stroked on.

Tin Man's armored limb swung out to meet him. The claw opened, ready to strike.

A wall of water moved, and the tiger shark was upon them, exploding out of the darkness.

Kaz went rigid, and the mechanical pincers missed him by inches. Clarence's titanic maw yawned open and snapped shut on Tin Man's aluminum plating. A single jagged tooth found a weak spot in the knee joint. It knifed between

THE DANGER

two pieces of metal, penetrating the suit's one-atmosphere seal.

There was a pop, and the weight of seven hundred feet of ocean blasted into Tin Man with the force of a battering ram. Marina never had a chance to scream. She was crushed to death in an instant.

A pectoral fin the size of a car door smacked into the empty tank on Kaz's back, sending him careening. By the time he'd recovered, his vision was darkening at the edges. He needed to breathe, needed it now. He could already feel himself slipping into a void far darker than the depths.

A thought came to him, one that he assumed would be his last: He had survived Tin Man, had even survived Clarence, only to suffocate just a few feet from the open hatch of the bell.

Something below him in the water was pushing him upward. With a burst of strength that was barely human, Menasce Gérard heaved him in through the work-lock. Limply, Kaz crashed to a pile of wet umbilicals on the curved floor.

Adriana and Dante yanked off his helmet.

Bobby Kaczinski took the sweetest breath he would ever remember.

08 September 1665

Captain James Blade came to regret his decision to have his Spanish prisoners put to death. This was not out of any sense of compassion. Rather, he now realized that he could have used them as slave labor to move the enormous treasure from Nuestra Señora *to the barque.*

The treasure. For the likes of Samuel Higgins, who had never held in his threadbare pockets more than a few coppers, the galleon's hold was the king's counting house. There could not possibly be more wealth in all the world. The gleaming silver pieces of eight made a mountain thrice the height of the tallest man aboard the Griffin. *There were enough gold bricks to build a palace. Pearls and gemstones spilled out of huge chests. Just the loose objects on the deck planking, lying where they had fallen like so much garbage, would have bought and sold empires.*

The gold bricks were the heaviest. Each one seemed to weigh four times what it should have, and even the smallest armload was almost too much for

THE DANGER

the exhausted and wounded privateers. Only forty men remained. Of their number, five were too grievously injured to work. One thing was certain, though. There would be no amputations now. York the barber had fallen in the battle for Nuestra Señora, a musket ball having pierced his heart.

Samuel thanked God that the bone-handled whip had been flung into the sea, for surely they all would have tasted it at some point during their labors. The work was slow, and the captain was not a patient man.

As the sun rose high over the yardarm and then began to set, Blade stood by the makeshift gangway that connected the Griffin to the much higher deck of the galleon. From that vantage point, he took stock of every coin and candlestick, cursing and berating the seamen who bore the burden of his newfound riches.

"Stir your stumps, you lice-ridden scum! I intend to be many days from here when the Spanish fleet comes looking for this rubbish barge!"

The captain would not even take the time to move the treasure below to the barque's hold, so anxious was he to be away. With the wealth of the East and the New World piled about the deck among coiled lines and water barrels, he gave the order to set fire to Nuestra Señora de la Luz.

Dusk was falling as the Griffin pulled away from

the blazing galleon. James Blade straddled his deck, chortling with triumph.

"Aye, Lucky is the name for you, boy. Fortune smiled upon me the day you came aboard this vessel."

A figure suddenly appeared amid the smoke of the burning ship. The Spaniard was not much older than Samuel, a cabin boy who had hidden himself deep in the galleon's many lower decks.

With a howl of defiance, the boy twirled a smoking ceramic firepot in a sling over his head. And then the flaming weapon was flung into the air, a streak of orange in the darkening sky. Every soul aboard the Griffin saw it, and yet it could not be stopped. It struck the deck not ten feet from Captain Blade and Samuel. As the earthenware pot shattered, the burning matchsticks ignited the packed gunpowder at its core.

There was a sharp report as the device exploded, spraying hot pitch in all directions. Cries of pain went up among the crew as the searing brimstone splashed onto exposed flesh. Samuel felt a hot stab on his beardless cheek. The captain bellowed in agonized fury.

As the embers flew, a single fleck of fiery sulfur found the collapsed area of deck in the barque's stern. Directly below were stored the ship's powder kegs.

THE DANGER

No attacking navy could have had the effect of that single speck of flame as it settled upon the volatile barrel stacked among two and twenty others.

The Griffin *blew herself to pieces. In a matter of seconds, Samuel found himself in the water. It was that sudden.*

Like most of the crew, he could not swim. He floundered in the waves, splashing wildly for just a few seconds before dipping beneath them.

This is it, then, *he thought.* What a strange place for an English climbing boy to end his life.

That life had not been a happy one. Yet as he sank deeper into the blackness, he realized wistfully how very much he wanted to live.

Suddenly, he was struck in the chest by a hard object rising from below. Instinctively, he clasped his arms around it, and it bore him upward. He broke to the surface, gasping and choking, and stared at the object that was keeping him afloat. It was a piece of the ship's carved figurehead, broken off in the explosion.

"Boy — Samuel! Over here!"

A short distance away, the captain flailed at the water in some semblance of swimming.

Samuel stared. There were no other cries for help, no struggling sailors. Of forty men, he and Blade were the only two left alive.

"*Samuel — hold on, lad, and kick your way over to me!*"

In this most dire of circumstances, Samuel thought of the murdered Spanish prisoners, the victims in Portobelo, the abused crew of the Griffin, *and of Evans the sail maker, who had died at this cruel man's hands.*

"*Hurry, boy! Your captain needs you!*"

Without hesitation, Samuel began to paddle in the opposite direction. He paid no attention to the volley of threats and oaths that were hurled after him. And when the tirade stopped, Samuel looked back and noted that James Blade had disappeared into the sea.

THE DANGER

CHAPTER EIGHTEEN

Dawn was breaking through the overcast as the storm moved off to Martinique and points east. Captain Bourassa and the skeleton crew aboard the *Adventurer* set about repairing the ship's fried electrical systems.

Star paced the deck like a caged tiger, her limp barely noticeable because of her speed and grim tension. It had been four hours since they had last been able to speak to the bell. And then the divers had been involved in a life-and-death struggle against an adversary in a half-ton suit.

"How soon till we get comms. back up?" she asked for the fifth time that hour.

Henri had the console open and was soldering burned wire. "No sooner for the asking so much," he replied, and added kindly, "English, he is the best. If anyone can bring home your friends — "

That was the problem, Star thought. *English was a great diver, but he wasn't all-powerful.*

If anything's happened to them, I'll never forgive myself for surviving!

DIVE

What a weird twist — that getting bent might have saved her life.

She bit back her impatience, and frowned as the *Ponce de Léon* approached out of the morning mist, and began to draw alongside. Through the haze, she could make out both Cutter and Reardon on deck.

A deep resentment welled up inside Star. Cutter had been the enemy from the beginning. Why trust him now? True, he had warned them about Marina. But what if that was a trick? A lift basket stuffed with a fortune hung dead in the water, somewhere below the *Adventurer*, waiting for power to be restored to the winch. Any piece of that load could be used as evidence in court for a treasure hunter to claim the wreck as his own.

At that moment, Star didn't know what ordeal her friends might have been through, or even if they were alive or dead. But she could be certain of this: They would never forgive her if she allowed their find to fall into the greedy hands of Tad Cutter.

She squinted at the winch, trying to size up the amount of cable wound around the wheel. Surely the basket wasn't too far beneath the surface now.

As she climbed the metal ladder down to the

THE DANGER

dive platform, the words of her doctor resounded in her ears: "You must never dive again. Another case of the bends, and you will surely be in a wheelchair for life."

Sorry, Doc, but this one's a must.

And she jumped into the sea.

Her fears disappeared the instant the water closed over her. How could anything that felt so right do her harm? She held her breath, descending effortlessly along the winch cable. She kept her eyes open, almost enjoying the stinging salt. The ocean was clear and quite bright despite the fact that the sun had not yet burned off the morning mist.

At last, the basket came into view, hanging at about forty feet. Her heart nearly stopped at the sight of it.

Oh, my God! I knew they found treasure, but this is the mother lode!

Silver turned black; pearls and gems faded. But gold was always gold. It was spectacular — something out of a fairy tale.

She grabbed a solid-gold candlestick and reached for a rope of pearls to wrap around her neck.

Her hand froze. *No. Just proof. Nothing more.* She kicked for the surface.

When she climbed back aboard, her exhilaration was total. No pain, no stiffness. Star Ling was a diver again.

She was sitting on the platform, catching her breath, when the lift bag broke the waves right where she had been swimming seconds earlier. Shouting for Henri, she took a boat hook from the rack and fished the bobbing float out of the water.

She gawked. Fastened by waterproof tape was a simple sandwich bag. Inside the clear plastic was a torn piece of paper bearing the message: TEAM OK. RAISE BELL.

Her heart soared. They were alive! Only —

How are we supposed to raise the pot without electricity?

And then Cutter appeared out of the haze, piloting a Zodiac inflatable over to the *Adventurer*.

He called, "What can we do to help?"

When the diving bell finally broke the surface, English and the three interns were astonished to find themselves deposited not onto their own ship, but to the deck of the *Ponce de Léon*.

What was going on here? They had narrowly escaped Marina only to be delivered right into the hands of Cutter and Reardon.

Luckily, Star was there to explain the situation through the intercom. "I think Cutter's our friend

THE DANGER

now, believe it or not. He's a treasure hunter and a reef wrecker, but he didn't know what Marina was doing. And when he found out, he warned us right away."

"Marina didn't make it," Kaz said soberly. He offered no details. It would be a while before he would be ready to discuss this particular adventure.

"Anyway, Cutter's giving us a ride over to the oil rig," Star concluded. "Captain Bourassa will meet us there. He's got to go slow over the reef because there's about a zillion dollars hanging under the *Adventurer*."

English glared at her through the small view port. "I hope you know this by *inference* only, mademoiselle with the wet hair, and not because you are foolish enough to dive there."

They were about halfway to the Antilles platform when the helicopters began to arrive, filling the sky with their machine-gun rhythms.

Dante peered out at them. "Big doings at the oil rig."

English laughed mirthlessly. "One billion dollars. Many zeroes attract many friends."

Adriana gaped at the aircraft that filled the skies over Saint-Luc like circling hawks. "You mean all this is for *us*?"

"I believe you Americans have a saying about — hitting the fan?"

The decompression from seven hundred feet took four long days. By the time the divers stepped out of the chamber, the contents of the lift basket and even Star's gold candlestick sat in the hold of a French warship that patrolled the waters over the wreck site at the edge of the Hidden Shoals.

Court claims on the treasure of *Nuestra Señora de la Luz* had been filed by Poseidon Oceanographic Institute, Antilles Oil, and three countries — France, England, and Spain.

Centuries after the days of the great treasure fleets, the same three governments were still bickering over Caribbean gold.

The claim filed on behalf of the four teenage interns, who had discovered not one but two seventeenth-century shipwrecks, was rejected by the International Maritime Commission.

Tad Cutter and Chris Reardon made no claim at all.

THE DANGER

CHAPTER NINETEEN

Kaz knocked on the door of the small cottage in the center of the village of Côte Saint-Luc.

English greeted the four interns and ushered them inside. "You leave tomorrow. This is what I hear, yes?"

Star grinned. "Poseidon has officially invited us to go home. Gallagher finally turned his back on the camera long enough to kick us out."

"Yeah," Dante said bitterly. "So he can hire lawyers to go after our billion dollars."

"Ah, the money." English dismissed this with a contemptuous shrug. "You are better off without it. It brings only complications."

"And private jets," Dante added feelingly.

"Two lives are lost," English reminded him. "No treasure is worth that."

"He knows," Kaz said gently. "He just wants to sulk. It's like therapy."

"We brought you a going-away present," Adriana announced.

English cast a disapproving glance at the enormous shopping bag that was being carried between Adriana and Star. "Then give it to someone who is going away. Me, I stay here."

"This one you're going to like," Adriana promised. She tore the bag away, revealing the wooden object she had found buried with the treasure at the wreck site. "It was the only thing the government didn't impound. They prefer gold, I guess."

English examined it with mild interest. "It is a carving," he observed. "Like the one I already have." He picked up the figure and turned it over in his arms. "The body and hindquarters of an animal. The head is missing."

"No, it isn't." Adriana was almost dancing with excitement. She crossed the small parlor and lifted the other piece from the fishnet hanging in the window. "The head is right here."

The dive guide frowned. "But this is impossible. The head is a bird. The body is some kind of beast."

"There's a mythological animal with the head and wings of an eagle and the body of a lion," Adriana explained. "It's a griffin. This artifact comes from the wreck of a ship called the *Griffin*."

Holding the eagle out in front of her, she walked up to English and lowered it on top of the

THE DANGER

carving in his arms. The jagged ends fit together like two puzzle pieces. One half was bleached by sun, the other blackened by centuries underwater. But there was no question that this had once been a single sculpture. Now it was whole again after more than three hundred years.

She stepped back and admired the effect. "This is the figurehead from the bow of the *Griffin*. If your ancestor floated ashore on part of it, then he was from that ship." She looked at him long and hard. "The *Griffin* was English, which means you are, too. Your family legend — it's all true."

Menasce Gérard was not often overwhelmed, but this was one of those times. At last, he managed, "You American teenagers — "

"I'm Canadian," Kaz reminded him.

"You bring me my history," the guide persisted. "I — I have no way to repay you."

Star regarded him solemnly. "I think saving our lives a thousand times probably counts."

English gazed at their faces as if committing each one to memory. "I will never forget you." The giant stood there for a moment awkwardly, and then opened his arms.

There was room for all four of them.

09 September 1665

Samuel came awake with the piece of the wooden figurehead still clutched in his arms, and the gritty taste of sand in his mouth. He shook himself and sat up, spitting and choking.

Alive! he thought. *He had not expected to be so.*

He took in his surroundings — a beach, palm trees, a pleasant floral scent on a tropical breeze.

An island.

Captain Blade was right about one thing, he thought. *I am lucky.*

He stood up, shaking with hunger and thirst, and spied a village just in from the beach. He could smell food cooking. Children played among the huts.

Now several people were heading his way. They resembled the natives Samuel had seen along the coastline around Portobelo. They reached him, exclaimed over him, brought him water.

"I'm English," he tried to explain, pointing to himself. "English."

They did not understand, nor could he make sense of their strange words. But the message of welcome

THE DANGER

was clear. The feeling that welled up inside him was something close to joy.

Samuel Higgins had never belonged anywhere. But this was a place where a young man could make a life for himself. Start a family.

Leave a legacy.

EPILOGUE

The X-ray machine at Martinique airport picked up the strange object in Star's duffel bag. Security officers swarmed from all directions. Star and her three traveling companions were pulled aside into the restricted area, and a search of the luggage began.

The agent in charge rummaged around the bag and pulled out the carved whalebone handle that had once belonged to Captain James Blade of His Majesty's privateer fleet.

"I totally forgot about that thing!" Star exclaimed.

And then the huge stone inset above the initials *J.B.* caught the light and flashed deep green fire at them. The interns stared at it, mouths agape. This was the first time they had seen it free of its encrustation of coral. It was magnificent.

A junior agent pointed urgently at the brilliant display. "Monsieur — *regardez!* The gem!"

With disinterested eyes, the inspector looked from the four teens in shorts to this huge garish stone.

THE DANGER

"Do not be ridiculous," he chided his subordinate. "It cannot be real. An emerald that size would be worth two million dollars!"

With a snort of disgust, he tossed the artifact back into Star's duffel, and passed the interns through.

"Souvenir tourist junk!"

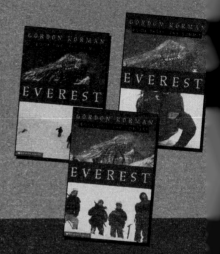
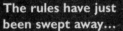